Finding Faith

Michelle Romano

Finding Faith
Copyright © 2018 Michelle Romano
ISBN: 978-1-98-208244-4

Revised 2023

All rights reserved.

No part of this book may be reproduced in any form or by any electronic or mechanical means, including information storage and retrieval systems, without written permission from the author, except for the use of brief quotations in a book review.

This book is a work of fiction. Names, characters, places, events, and incidents are either products of the author's imagination or are used fictitiously. Any similarity to actual persons, living or dead, events or locales is entirely coincidental.

Sometimes, Faith is all we have.

Acknowledgements

I want to express deep gratitude to Marjie Kyriopoulos, author, dear friend, and my soul sister for editing this revision of *Finding Faith*.

I'm deeply grateful to Lawrence Bergum who taught me about unconditional love and the importance of showing up for ourselves so we can show up for others.

I'm thankful to my best friend, Kari Ann Windorpski, for always loving and supporting me.

I'm indebted to my parents, both of whom have applauded my efforts as a writer. My mom encouraged me to keep journals as a child, which fueled my energy for writing. She is an inspiration through her endless devotion, love and generosity. My dad is a phenomenal listener and storyteller. As an author himself, he continues to provide support and guidance.

Sometimes it takes a village. Thank you for being in my village.

Faith

Chapter 1

The candle's flame pulled me in. I was captivated by its hypnotic dance. The world receded, my vision narrowed, and all I saw was the glow of the light.

The Vintage, an old and restored house converted into a bar nestled in the Cobble Hill neighborhood of Brooklyn, displayed candle sconces and tea lights. It was the perfect place to hide from life for a while.

My only friend Terese, sat across from me. We had met two years ago on the train, struck up a conversation and soon became friends. When I mentioned that I was looking for a job, she hired me at her advertising firm. Meeting at The Vintage had become our weekly ritual.

"Hey, you alright Faith? Maybe you should go somewhere to get away," Terese suggested.

"Yeah," I murmured, unable to form a clear thought, still distracted by the candlelight. My breath was shallow, my will to connect to the world, gone.

"Well, I think you should . . ."

I barely heard her and nodded without emotion.

"Shall we go or are you still sippin' your drink?" Her Brooklyn accent conveyed a hint of impatience. We'd been sitting for well over an hour and she was itching to see my bubbly self return.

I slurred, "I'd like to stay. You can go." It was too hard to do much of anything, let alone talk.

Terese bent down, gave me a hug and left. I felt solace in being alone and I was drawn back to the flame.

∽ ∽

My world had crumbled on a Sunday morning. After having gone to bed with *him*, I awoke to find myself alone. I called his name and my voice was met with silence. I ran through the kitchen and the bathroom, and then I dashed back into the bedroom. I opened his dresser drawers. They were empty. All his belongings had vanished. Reality hammered me. My body shook and my stomach heaved while the room spun. I didn't know what to do. Daniel was gone.

Collapsing on the couch, I sobbed. *How could this happen? He vowed he would never leave.* Through tears, desperately searching for answers, I looked around the living room. A small piece of paper was taped to the doorframe leading to the kitchen. My head spun as I rose to read it.

This isn't working for me. I'm leaving – Daniel.

I turned the paper over. It was blank. I read his words over and over to see if I had missed something. *Did he fall out of love with me? Was there another woman or was he just not capable of commitment?*

Almost three months had passed since that dreary October morning, yet it felt as though it was just yesterday. Sometimes, I smelled his musky cologne in the closet and loving feelings rushed back. Other times, a hot ball of anger pounded inside me. I spent most of my waking hours sitting in front of my bedroom window desperately anticipating the sight of his black pickup truck, certain it would roll down the street and stop in front of our apartment. I waited for Daniel to knock on the door, pleading for me to take him back and confessing that he'd made the worst mistake of his life.

Even though life moved around me, I stood still. I felt no hunger pangs or thirst. I was numb and had checked out. From that awful day forward, I had attempted to fit the pieces together and analyze why this had happened, in some futile hope that, if I could find the reason for the breakup, I could fix whatever was broken.

I recalled how he had come home late from work several times without an explanation. He also hadn't invited me to attend work functions. One time, I smelled sweet perfume on his business shirt. There were other things too, but I couldn't remember . . .

The server interrupted my thoughts. "Would you like another drink?"

Jarred back to the real world, I muttered, "No." My face was wet with tears. Terese had left an hour ago. Looking up, I wiped my cheeks and glanced around the room. Most patrons were busy chatting. But, in the corner of the bar, there was a tall man with dirty blonde hair dining alone.

Our eyes met for a brief moment. My heart fluttered. Looking behind me to see if his gaze was for someone else, I saw no one. When my eyes returned to his table, he was gone.

I paid my bill and walked home. Light snow covered my footprints.

The next day, when I stepped out of the shower, the answering machine was blinking. My heart began to race. *Could it be Daniel?*

I pushed play and heard a familiar voice. "Faith, I booked you a one-way e-ticket to Hill City, Arizona leaving Saturday afternoon. When you arrive, look for a blue taxi. The driver will take you to a cottage. I'm heading out of town for work, but I will talk with you soon. Love you."

Chapter 2

When the plane landed, I collected my bags and found the blue taxi to take me to the location that Terese had booked. It was a forty-minute drive south of the Flagstaff airport, near the Coconino National Forest. On the way, I saw desert with layers of red sedimentary rock. Prickly green cacti with bright white and yellow flowers stood tall in the rugged dirt. My jitters flying across the country calmed when I saw this enchanting place. It felt strangely familiar as I watched the scenery from the back seat of the car. After a while, the cab came to a halt on a ledge overlooking canyons with the same red rock.

The crisp air startled me as I gathered my luggage. Bundling the scarf around my neck and hugging the sides of my jacket to stay warm, I stopped and stared at the cottage in front of me. It looked as though it had been plucked out of the Scottish Highlands and plopped on the outskirts of this small town. Faded brown boxes of colorful pansies and petunias lined the windows. A porch wrapped around the home. It reminded me of a house in a childhood fairy tale.

Luckily, the cottage was unlocked. A heavy, brass key hung on a hook on an inside wall. I closed the door, dropped my bags and sighed. I walked into a calm, beige living room with just enough furniture. There was an inviting couch, a Tiffany floor lamp, and a small stereo. The tiny kitchen was well stocked. Flour, sugar, and baking supplies lined the counter tops. Spices, cereals, soups, and boxed foods were inside the cupboards. Ideas for recipes poured into my mind. The refrigerator had orange juice, a carton of milk, butter, eggs, and celery. A bowl of fresh fruit was on the counter. *Terese must have arranged this days ago.*

Exhausted, I walked into the bedroom and plopped onto the king size bed. It felt soft and warm. Something about this place nudged the back of my mind, but I was too tired to remember. I closed my eyes for just a moment.

That minute turned into a long, restless night. I tossed and twisted, dreaming of Daniel. When I awoke, my face was damp with tears. Even with sleep, I couldn't find relief.

It was dark outside when I walked onto the back porch. Millions of sparkling stars blanketed the sky. I wanted a sign that this was where I was supposed to be, if only for a short time. Then I saw a shooting star.

I went back inside, lay down on the bed, and stared at the ceiling. Soon, I was asleep.

I woke up early in the morning and looked outside. The sky was beginning to lighten and slowly spread open. As I stepped into the shower, the phone rang. I ran to answer it.

"Hello?" My voice cracked.

"Faith? It's Terese. I wanted to make sure you made it safely. How are you?" I heard the worry in her voice.

I cleared my throat. "Good morning." The initial elevation in my voice plummeted. "It's early here."

"Oh, no. I forgot about the time difference. I'm sorry. Did I wake you? It's 10:00 a.m. here. I can call back, if you'd like," Terese said.

"It's okay. I'm up already. I didn't sleep well. But this place is amazing. How did you ever find it? Have you been here before? Thank you so much for your gift. I've never done anything like this before."

"Slow down, and catch your breath," Terese playfully teased. "I'm so glad you're there. I used to travel to Flagstaff for work and, after searching the internet, I found that cottage in Hill City. You'll have to check out the town. I read online that there are cute shops, a restaurant and a movie theater. I'm sorry if you felt rushed to go, but I knew if I hadn't done this soon, you might never have gone. Now listen, all expenses are paid for you for the next two months."

"You're wonderful. Thanks so much for everything. We'll have to find time for you to visit. By the way, something feels very familiar about this place . . ."

Chapter 3

After my phone call with Terese, I finished showering, dressed, drank a warm cup of tea and went outside. It was good to see sunlight and smell the fresh desert air.

My little cottage was perched on a slope overlooking an expanse of desert that stretched for miles. Cacti sprouted flowers and agave plants were sculpted, so different from sights in New York City.

The wind swept over the hills and through a maze of cacti and pinyon pine trees. Birds sang in the distance.

As I walked down the trail and into the valley, something made me stop. My nostrils filled with a familiar, sweet, yet disturbing fragrance. The smell reminded me of the scent on Daniel's shirt. I tried to take in deep breaths, but my lungs felt tight. The pressure on my chest paralyzed my body. I stumbled onto a small patch of grass and was suddenly on my back, looking at the clear sky.

I lay there for some time before I was able to focus on

how I was really feeling. Peacefulness surrounded me, softening the weight and draining my sorrow. But this sudden stillness brought back painful memories I had been trying to push out of my mind. Instead of hiding from the pain, the silence forced me to face it all over again.

After what felt like an eternity, I mustered the energy to stand up. I walked slowly back to the cottage, made a simple lunch and felt better.

∽ ∾

I had stopped jogging after that dreadful Sunday when I awoke alone. That was months ago.

I began my first run on a chilly Monday morning early in February, one week after my arrival. I picked my favorite eighties playlist on my iPod. With each beat of music, I quickened my step until I was in tempo. Even though the breeze tried to blow me back, I pushed through the gusts, following the curves on the uphill path.

My breathing came hard and fast at first, but as I ran, it gradually subsided into an even rhythm. Sweat dripped down my forehead while the sun beat on my head. I pounded my feet into the ground, hoping the pain and anger would exit through the soles of my shoes and seep deep into the earth. My arms pumped like pistons, helping to propel me over the hills. I felt a release of stress and tension that came from running. More importantly, I could leave my thoughts behind as my mind cleared.

After my run, I walked into town. No one knew me there. I had no car and didn't need one. Most places were within half a mile from my new home.

I went to Betty's Restaurant. My stomach growled. A bell chimed when I opened the door. I sat down on a bar stool at the ice cream counter and admired the small knick-knacks and colorful miniature toy antiques that lined the walls. A tall fan blew in the direction of an old wind chime. I was mesmerized by its echoing bells. There were so many ice cream flavors—toasted coconut, white chocolate raspberry, mint chocolate chip and more. I couldn't decide if that was what I wanted, so I glanced at the menu.

A thin, middle-aged woman behind the counter walked over. She had dimples and straight bright, red hair that fell halfway down her back.

"Hi there. Name's Betty. What can I get ya?" Gum snapped in her mouth.

"I'll have a small salad and some water." I hadn't had a salad since I arrived in Hill City.

"Alrighty, then. You new around here? I haven't seen you before."

"Yes, I'm Faith. I'm from New York City."

"New York, eh? I've always wanted to go there and see the Big Apple. We move slower around here. It's God's Country." Her big blue eyes peered over her red-rimmed glasses.

I tried to smile. "I like it so far."

"I'm glad." She whisked away and called out my order.

This positive energy was contagious. I was glad I had left behind my urban lifestyle.

Betty brought me the salad and water. I ate slowly, savoring every bite. After lunch, I went into the local drug store to get pens and stationery. People seemed friendly, but I felt like I was being watched as I wandered up and down the aisles.

"You new around here, I reckon?" A man who was

probably in his late sixties stood behind the counter. He wore baggy, torn, blue jeans and a white shirt that hung loosely outside his pants.

"Yes, I am. My name's Faith." I placed the pens and stationery on the counter.

"I see," he said, glaring at me. "It's about *time* you came back," his voice deepened. He walked away when an older woman put down the dollar bills she was counting and quickly went over to him.

"Harold, come on now. Where are your manners?" Turning to face me, she asked, "Faith, is it?" She stared hard at him and looked at me with a grin.

"Er, um, yes."

"Please excuse Harold. He's . . . confused," she whispered. She rang up my items, and gave me the receipt.

"Oh ok, thank you and have a nice day."

I looked down as I walked toward the door. Suddenly, I tripped and bumped into someone. When I looked up, I saw a tall, handsome man with a silly smirk on his face. He looked vaguely familiar. Heat spread across my cheeks.

"Oh, I'm so sorry."

"You all right, missy?" he boomed.

I was so flustered I couldn't find words. On top of that, I couldn't place how I knew him.

"Ah, yes, thank you," I said, my face glued to the ground as I quickly walked past him.

Chapter 4

After a couple weeks of rest and solitude, I decided to stay in Hill City indefinitely. There was no reason to return to New York City. Starting a new life here felt like a good next step. Even though Terese was covering all my expenses for one more month, I'd been thinking about getting a job in town. The idea of helping others always made me feel good and I needed to fill my time with something productive to get out of the house. I knew just the place to look for work. I walked into town on a mission.

"Ahem," I said, approaching the desk at St. Lucille's Nursing Home.

The middle-aged man behind the counter jumped.

"I didn't mean to startle you."

He turned around and brushed his dark brown hair out of his eyes. "That's okay. It's nap time for us so it's quiet this time of day. Do I know you?"

I opened my mouth, started to say something and

stopped. He looked familiar. He was handsome with dark European features.

"Um, no," I managed. My face felt warm. "My name is Faith. I'm from New York City and I'm looking for a job. Are you hiring?"

"Ah . . . I don't know. My name is Leo." He stared at me, ducked behind the counter and reappeared holding an application in his trembling hands. "Here, fill this out and bring it by, ah, Monday around noon. Gayle, our general manager, should be in then and you can talk with her."

I glanced at his name badge. It read Assistant Manager. "Thank you so much, Leo. I'll come back in a few days." I turned around and headed for the door. *That was awkward. Why did he look familiar?* I dismissed my curiosity, chalking it up to him having one of those typical faces.

As I left St. Lucille's, I admired the brown, brick building with small windows. At the front entrance, there was a small, gurgling water fountain surrounded by a garden of colorful flowers. A wreath made of tiny dried red flowers decorated the main door.

When I got home, I filled out the application. I'd never worked in a nursing home before but I'd always been fond of the elderly.

I changed into jogging pants and went for a run in the valley. As I circled the path in a warm up jog, a shadow appeared around the bend. It was an older woman dressed in long, white, neatly pressed slacks and a pale blue loose-fitting shirt. Slowing my pace, I approached her and she turned around. She was short and looked as though she was in her late seventies. Her long silver hair was tied in a bun.

"Hi," I said, walking towards her.

"Hi." She smiled, curiosity in her eyes. "You must

be new around here. I haven't seen you before," she added, as if this was the most commonly rehearsed line in town.

"Yes, I'm from New York City."

"Oh?"

"I've been here for a couple of weeks. I decided to relocate here, and I just applied for a job this morning."

"Oh, good for you. Where if I may ask?"

"At St. Lucille's, the nursing home in . . ."

"Oh yes, of course. I know where that is. My husband lives there." Her green eyes lit up. "Oh, heavens, where are my manners? I forgot to introduce myself. I'm Gracie."

"Nice to meet you, Gracie. My name is Faith." We shook hands.

Gracie stood silent for a few moments, as if she had a profound thought.

"What a beautiful name. Who did you talk with at St. Lucille's?"

"I spoke with Leo who told me to come back on Monday to speak with Gayle."

Gracie suddenly turned pale and started shaking.

"Are you alright? Would you like to sit down?" I found the nearest bench and we sat down.

"Oh, that's better. I'm fine now. Thank you, my dear. As I was trying to say, my husband, Lance, lives at the nursing home. I'm going to visit him today. I'll put in a good word for you. I hope you get the job. It would be nice to get to know you."

"Thank you. That's kind of you. If I get the job, I'll look for you."

After a few minutes, Gracie said she had to go. I offered to walk with her to make sure she felt well enough to get home safely, but she politely turned me down, stating she felt much better.

※ ※

When I arrived home, there was a message on my answering machine. It was Terese. She invited me to New York City over Valentine's weekend. She said she would buy my ticket. I called her immediately.

"Hey, it's Faith."

"Hi! I'm glad to hear from you. Did you get my message?" she asked, breathing deeply. "I'm sorry, I barely made it inside when I heard the phone ring."

"Is something wrong?"

"Oh, no. I just came back from the store. I miss you and want to see you again."

Since she had offered to pay for my trip, I decided to go. Anything beats being alone on Valentine's Day.

"Alright, you've convinced me." I wanted to tell her about staying in Hill City and the job application, but I decided to wait and have that conversation in person.

※ ※

When Terese and I saw each other at the airport, we practically jumped into each other's arms. It felt great to hug her.

"It's so good to see you, Faith!"

"Ditto!" I got my bag and headed for her Jeep.

"I know your time here is short, so let's grab lunch and chat about things." Terese drove to a small café in the quaint neighborhood of Cobble Hill.

We sat at a table and ordered burgers, fries and sodas.

"So, first tell me how you're doing," Terese beamed.

"I'm alright. It's lonely in Hill City, I won't lie about

that. But I feel like I'm starting to heal." I looked at her. "And, I like Hill City so much that I would like to stay."

"What do you mean *stay?*" I could see the wheels turning in her head.

"Live there, indefinitely."

"Wow! Are you sure you're making the right decision? This was supposed to be a temporary getaway," Terese said.

I couldn't contain my excitement. The more I thought about uprooting my life and staying in Hill City, the more delighted I became. "I'd like to extend my stay at the cottage. I already applied for a job at a nursing home," I said, grinning.

"Sounds like you have things all figured out. I'll talk with the owner but I know the cottage has been vacant."

I smiled. Although I'd miss seeing her at work every day, in my gut, I felt this was the right decision.

"Well, I would certainly miss seeing you. Things will be different without you. But I know you've been going through a lot lately. I didn't think you'd move across the country, but I support you if this is what you want to do," Terese said.

"Thanks for trying to understand. I know it sounds weird, but I feel comfortable in Hill City."

Terese nodded. "I'm glad."

I added, "I hired a mover and need my things shipped to Hill City. When Daniel left, I got rid of a lot of stuff and packed up most of my things in boxes, hoping that one day I'd move. This day came sooner than I anticipated but that's okay. If you could help let the movers into the apartment, I'd really appreciate it. They will arrive next weekend."

"Sure, I'll take care of it. I still have a key for your place. So, since this may be your last time in New York City for a while, let's go out and have fun! Work has been so stressful lately. Let's find action." She winked, and I knew what she meant.

"I'm game." It would be nice to go out on the town.

∞ ∞

Once we got to her condo in Queens, we got dressed up. Terese braided my hair, and I curled hers. She let me wear her long-sleeved, short black V-neck dress with warm black tights and dark red high-heeled boots. She wore black pants, a tight red top and black high-heeled boots.

We bundled up with coats, hats and mittens, and then hailed a cab. Once we were in the car, Terese asked, "So, what if we pretend to be someone else tonight? What do you think?"

"Yeah, that sounds like a great idea." Being back in New York City brought back painful memories but it also reminded me of how silly we could be together. "So who are you going to be? And what about me and my back-story?"

"I always liked the name Zoey." Terese turned to get my reaction.

"Ok, I want my name to be Allie."

Terese nodded and said, "The only rule is we don't babysit each other. If we meet a couple of men, let's meet up before we leave to chat about what's going on, so we won't worry."

It hadn't dawned on me that Terese assumed that I might meet a man. Thinking we would just have a good time dancing; I wasn't sure I had it in me to attract a man after Daniel. Terese hadn't been with a man for a very long time. She was on the prowl for a steamy evening.

⸺ ⸺

We got to Gaby's Nightclub twenty minutes later. Inside, it was dark and packed. Most people were on the dance floor. We scooted over to a vacant high-top table and sat across from each other. Terese ordered a mojito and I ordered champagne.

Dance music jammed in the background. We scanned the dance floor and then the bar. I was slightly buzzed, when I saw a tall muscular man with black hair, walking over to our table. I assumed he was coming for Terese, so I didn't pay attention to him.

When he extended his hand, asking me to dance, I looked wide-eyed at Terese. She motioned for me to go with him and mouthed, "Wow."

Smiling shyly, I followed him to the floor, which was so crowded we barely had room to dance.

The man dipped down to my ear and yelled, "Hi, I'm Cole! What's your name?"

"Allie!" The light hit him just right. I saw his piercing blue eyes. Cole smiled and began swaying to the music. His Polo cologne was intoxicating. Once we were moving rhythmically together, I let loose on the dance floor, something I hadn't done in a long time. *Damn! This feels good!*

Terese was dancing with a shorter guy. She looked like she was having fun.

The songs thumped in my chest. A woman who had too much to drink pushed Cole into me. Stumbling back, I grabbed his shoulders and my fingers glided over his muscles.

When the music slowed, Cole took my hand and led me to our table to retrieve my winter gear. We strolled to the back of the bar and agreed to use the bathroom before we headed out. I ran into Terese.

"Hey you!" I yelled. The music vibrated.

"Hi! Fancy seeing you. I'm heading home with someone I met. Have a good time and I'll see you later," Terese said, winking at me. She hugged me and quickly left.

I found Cole. Looking into those mysterious blue eyes, I felt a bolt of electricity. He smiled, grabbed my hand and led me outside.

"Man, it's so loud and crowded in there! I know a place where we can go to talk."

I stopped walking, wondering if I should go with this stranger. I set my fears aside, nodded in agreement, and followed his lead.

"So, where are you from?" he asked as we walked on the dark cobblestone street.

I was unprepared to have an actual conversation with a hunk from a bar until I remembered I was pretending to be someone else tonight. I hugged my jacket in the cold weather.

"New York City." I didn't want to stray too far from the truth.

"Very cool."

We walked the rest of the way in an awkward silence. *What's his story? He could've had any of the women in the bar and he chose me.*

We stopped at a rusty old metal door. He turned to me and whispered, "Come with me. Wait till you see this."

Noticeably, I had a little too much to drink. I couldn't

walk straight. We climbed the stairs to the roof. As we got near the side of the building, I had the fleeting thought that he could throw me over the edge at any moment. Instead, he pointed to the vast city that spread out before us.

"Wow, I've never been up here before," I managed to say. For an instant, it reminded me of Hill City. We could see some stars and it was quieter up here than it was on the street below.

I was shivering so Cole led me into a heated gazebo. *There's an actual gazebo up here?*

Cole gently pushed me against the wall. I felt Cole's weight shift and he guided my chin up to his face. I searched his eyes.

"Where have you been all my life?" he asked, pulling me closer, inviting me to smell the alcohol on his breath.

He was handsome in his trendy clothes and seemed out of my league. I reminded myself that he was probably hammered and I shouldn't believe a word he said. Furthermore, my life had no room for a man. Still, I hadn't been on a date since Daniel and I wanted to know if I could be with a guy like Cole.

While I was thinking all of this, Cole's warm mouth dipped down and closed around mine. He pulled my head toward his and waves of electricity circulated in my body. His tongue edged its way into my mouth, gently probing every corner. I surrendered, and leaned into him, pelvis first. In response, his rock-hard manhood pressed into me.

Lost in a trance, I felt Cole take off my coat and boots and slide down my tights. Between kisses, our breaths were hard and fast. Cole reached inside my dress for my ripe nipples and caressed each breast. I moaned. While Cole kissed me, I felt his jeans fall to the ground, covering my feet. Slowly and gently, he tilted me back and laid me down on a chaise lounge next to the wall of the gazebo. He rested on top of me searching desperately for a way inside. I grabbed his body and felt him slide into me as he groaned with satisfaction. His energy penetrated throughout my body and soul, unlocking my gates of steel and filling me with ultimate pleasure. Only then did I realize I was ready to be with someone new.

    I must've fallen asleep, because when I awoke a couple hours later, Cole was gone. Next to me was a deep red rose and a small Valentine card with two words: *Be Mine.*

Chapter 5

The plane landed and all I could think about was that fiery night with Cole. I had an aching memory of him inside me. *Maybe it would've been nice to get to know him a little better.*

I arrived in Hill City Sunday evening. I was thankful to be home.

Monday came quickly. I walked into St. Lucille's and saw a dozen elderly men and women sitting on chairs and sofas, all facing a window. They looked as lost as I felt when I first arrived in Hill City.

A plump woman, who seemed to be in a position of authority, looked up when I approached the desk. Her hazel eyes lit up.

"Oh, you must be Faith. I've heard a lot of great things about you from Gracie. My name is Gayle. I hear you're interested in working here. Do you have any experience working in a nursing home?"

I hadn't thought about my experience related to senior

care and politely replied, "No, I don't, but I'd be interested in learning more about . . ."

"Well, if you're interested, you could work part-time socializing with the residents." She paused, looked at me, and said, "Yes, that's exactly what we need. What do you think?"

Suddenly, doubt struck me. *Is it too soon? Am I ready to jump in? Will people like me? Can I learn this job?*

She didn't ask me about my job experience in New York City. Maybe it was the small-town culture.

Pushing my fears aside, I said, "Sounds really good."

"Great!" Gayle walked briskly to the other side of the desk and gave me a welcome hug.

My body tingled. I was so caught up in the moment, I hadn't realized that the application had not yet left my hand. I put it on the counter.

Grinning, Gayle asked, "So, can you start now?"

"Yes," I beamed.

"For your first few days, I'd like you to interact with the residents to get to know them and hear their stories. Everyone has a story to share."

Gayle walked down the corridor and gestured for me to follow. "We value the gift of life here. As sad as it is, everyone passes on. So, while our residents are in our community, we have the opportunity to make their last few years meaningful. They may be forgetful or old, but that doesn't devalue their humanity. We view our work as being in service to our elders and we believe in honoring them for all they've given to us. We are fortunate to be with them as they grow older and we want to make sure they have a kind hand to hold in the last years of their lives."

Tears pricked my eyes. Gayle's perspective further convinced me that I had landed the perfect job.

I stopped walking when I saw residents gazing out of a window.

"Oh, we call that the magic glass. You'll quickly learn this is a favorite place to sit. We've heard all kinds of stories about what they see in this window," Gayle said with a soft smile.

That first day at St. Lucille's, I mingled with a few residents. If they didn't feel like talking, I simply sat beside them. After a few hours, I went home filled with a renewed sense of purpose. For the first time in a long while, I slept soundly.

The next day, when I started my shift, I had a list of patients to visit. While I was walking down the hall and making notes on a clipboard, I nearly bumped in to Gracie. She teetered and reached for my arm.

"Oh, Gracie, I'm so sorry."

"Oh, dear, that's quite alright. You didn't see me and I should've said something to catch your attention, but I was thinking about something else. Don't you worry. I'm fine."

"I've been trying to bump into you, but not like this," I joked. "So, where are you off to?"

"I was just leaving to go home and take a nap but I'll be back later to see my Lance." Before I could reply, I saw her expression change. "Hey, if you're still around in a couple of hours, why don't you join Lance and me?"

"Oh, that would be lovely." I waved goodbye.

The next couple of hours passed quickly. I walked to Lance's room and peeked in. Gracie sat by her husband's bedside, gazing into his eyes and blowing him kisses. I felt the tremendous love they held for each other as I knocked gently, trying not to interrupt.

Gracie looked up. "Why, Faith, do come in. Lance, darling, this is Faith."

Lance slowly turned his face to look at me. We hadn't been formally introduced.

"Hello there, Lance," I said.

"Well hello, Faith." He smiled.

Lance looked twenty years older than Gracie. He was a gentle man, in and out of lucidity due to his dementia, and unable to take care of himself without assistance. A long white robe hugged his body.

"So, how did you two meet?" I asked.

"We met at a barn dance years ago. I walked over and started talking with Lance. Everyone looked at me like I was nuts. Back then, the woman never made the first move. But at that point, I didn't care. I just knew we were meant to be together."

"How did you know?" I asked.

"I just knew. I felt something when he looked at me." Gracie smiled.

Lance turned to Gracie and said, "We're still very much in love after all these years."

Oh, how I want to find something that amazing!

"Faith, you remind me of someone I knew. She was remarkable." Lance's voice brought me back to the room.

Suddenly, Gracie looked at her watch, "Oh, my, it's getting late and you have to get to sleep, Lance."

She quickly turned to me. "Thank you so much for giving us some company tonight. We had a delightful time, didn't we, darling?"

"Of course we did. We'll have to meet again soon," Lance said.

Gracie steered me towards the door.

"Thanks. I had a wonderful time and look forward to talking with you both again."

I retreated, wondering what Lance meant when he said I reminded him of someone and why Gracie was pushing me out the door.

As I walked home that night, I felt less depressed. I enjoyed being at St. Lucille's. I admired the residents' ability to celebrate life and felt inspired by their stories. The lines on their faces reflected the passage of time and the accumulation of wisdom.

When I got home, I fell into bed, exhausted. As the wind blew in through the screen, I closed my eyes, had a few fleeting thoughts of Cole, and fell asleep.

∞ ∞

A few weeks later, on a cloudy morning late in March, I didn't have to be at work until mid-afternoon.

I meditated and reflected on my journey, struck by how difficult it was to remember parts of my life. I simply drew a blank. *Am I that old? Have I been too distracted? How had I not noticed this earlier?*

In many ways, my life reminded me of the residents' lives. I was regularly bumping into people who looked familiar but I couldn't remember anything beyond that. After Daniel left, I became more vulnerable to illness. My entire body had grown weak and tired, my spirit broken, submerged beneath layers of sorrow, mistrust and self-pity.

But now, there was a feeling of renewed strength. I hadn't felt this well in a long time. I would no longer allow Daniel or anyone else to have such control over my life.

Being around the elderly was a daily reminder to be thankful for the miles I'd traveled in my own life. After my meditation, I walked to St. Lucille's for my afternoon shift. Once there, I put my coat in the workroom. I had to start work in twenty minutes, so I went to the magic window where the residents sat, gazing out, and I took a seat. I closed my eyes and listened to their quiet conversations.

I took two deep breaths and concentrated on relaxing as I felt the sun on my brow. I opened my eyes to gaze through the crystal-clear window, a gateway to the outside world. Rarely did family members or friends come to visit the residents, which tore at my heart. It almost made me want to move in.

While immersed in my thoughts, a sweet old lady sat next to me and said softly, "Faith, is it?"

"Yes," I said, surprised that she knew my name.

"You're absolutely beautiful. It's so good that you came home. We've missed you."

Chapter 6

I had been working at the nursing home for over a month. Each day when the residents talked, I heard their lives unfold in stories and these became gifts of wisdom. My understanding of old age had altered completely.

There was one woman in her early nineties who held my attention from the beginning. She never made eye contact and she always looked so sad.

One Friday night in early April, I was almost done working. Most of the residents were already asleep, except for this woman who sat by the magic window with her hands placed on her lap, palms up. I sat down next to her and closed my eyes.

A few minutes later, she spoke. "I've endured great joy and profound sadness in my lifetime, feelings so powerful they're lodged within my heart and still cause pain, even after so many years. It was bittersweet. I fell in love with an older man, an incredible soul. He helped children every day. He was almost perfect."

It sounded as if she was talking to me, but I wasn't sure. I didn't move.

"I remember holding his hands. I adored his hands. Though weathered and worn, they were gentle and strong. His mouth curved into a big smile when he was happy. Tears fell from his eyes when he was sad. His strong scent lifted me to the high heavens and back. I remember the hold he had on me whenever he was near. It has yet to fade, after all these years." She quietly cried.

I couldn't believe she was sharing this with me. I didn't open my eyes for fear of breaking the mood. The story melted into me like a warm cup of tea.

"When I kissed him, I flew up to the moon and back, but he stayed on earth. I held his hand in mine, feeling his warmth, yet his emotions were buried so deep that it was impossible to reach inside and find a way for us to merge as one."

It sounded as though she was narrating a story. This woman was usually quiet, but today, she had a lot to say.

"He confessed his love for me, but I couldn't feel it. Maybe he was too tired to fight for me. Maybe that was what it was . . . Maybe that was what it was," she said again, as though attempting to understand her own pain.

I finally understood why she looked so sad. Her heart had been broken, much like mine had. Tears streamed down her face. Maybe this was the first time she had shared her story.

After a while, she whispered, "I'm tired."

I helped her up, walked with her to her room and eased her into bed. She was asleep a minute later. I sat down and watched her breathe and twitch as she was taken deep down into a place where there were no broken hearts.

The more I thought about her story, the sadder I became. I knew how difficult it was to be in love with someone who couldn't reciprocate love in the same way. Without thinking, I closed my eyes and fell asleep.

When I awoke, I wondered where I was. The clock on the bed stand read 3:00 a.m.. This woman who had opened her heart to me was still sound asleep. She looked peaceful. It was the most serene I had seen her. Slowly and gently, I pulled the covers over her and walked out of the room and into the staff lounge.

"Faith, what are you doing here so early?"

I jumped. "Oh, hi, Marjie. You scared me. I was with one of the residents down the hall. When I tucked her in, I fell asleep." Marjie was the veteran nurse on the night shift.

She nodded. "You must be tired. Why don't you take my car and go home to sleep? I'll be here when you come in for your shift later."

"That's so nice. Thank you."

With my eyes half open, I don't know how I made it home. Exhausted, I fell right into bed, uniform and all.

∽ ∾

Later that morning, I woke up feeling refreshed. Then, I recalled the conversation with that woman and how I'd forgotten to look for her name. I remembered Marjie was waiting for her car, so I dressed and hurried into work.

I wanted to check on the woman I'd met last night, but I couldn't recall which room was hers. I gradually got busier making my rounds.

"Faith." A finger tapped my shoulder while I drank a

cup of hot tea in the break room. I turned around in a daze. It was Matt, an older nurse in his sixties.

"Hi, Matt," I yawned. "What's up?"

"I have to leave, so Gayle asked if you could check on my last patient."

"Sure. I'd love to. Just tell me where to go." I took another sip of tea.

"Her name is Rose and she's the third door on the right. Thank you so much," he said, pointing down the hall, as he grabbed his coat and left.

When I got to the room, I noticed this was the room where I'd been the night before. On the door was her name: Rose. It had been too dark to see the nameplate last night.

Rose was taking a nap. I went over to her bed and saw that she had difficulty breathing. Many of the residents had respiratory complications.

I sat in a large chair next to her bed. Rose wore a white summer dress laced with red roses and like the night before, her palms lay open. I closed my eyes.

After a little while, I heard a slight movement and remembered I was on duty. I glanced over at Rose. Her big blue eyes looked back at me, first with a sense of hesitation and then with comfort.

"Hello," she said sleepily.

"Hi, Rose. My name is Faith. How are you feeling today?"

For a few minutes, she looked at me with wide eyes. Her irises were various shades of blue. Her face shadowed some sadness, but I also saw peace I hadn't seen before when she was awake.

Finally, she said, "Tired. I'm feeling really tired today."

"Me, too. Close your eyes and sleep some more," I suggested, trying to soothe her.

"I'd like that. You look tired. You can go and I'll go to sleep," she slurred in a whisper.

When I was almost at the door, Rose said, "I forgot to tell you, his name was Ron."

I left, feeling a connection with Rose. There was more to learn about her.

Two days later, the phone rang.

"Faith, this is Gayle, I have some bad news."

I braced myself.

"Rose died in her sleep this morning. There was nothing anyone could do to save her," she blurted.

I stood in shock and denial.

"I know this is difficult, because you cared about her," she said, trying to comfort me.

"Oh, my God." My heart fell.

"The funeral will be here tomorrow. We would love it if you could come in, even though it's your day off," she added.

"Yes, of course, I'll be there." I hung up the phone. There was a lump in my throat. This was surreal.

Sadness swept over me. I wanted to learn more from Rose. I needed to understand what made love tick and why it still hurt so much. Now, I was left wondering about the passionate details of the love affair she had cherished.

People of all ages dressed in black filled the chapel. In the middle of the sanctuary lay Rose's shiny wooden casket.

I took a seat in the back of the room, watching people filter in, some crying. Once everybody sat down, a priest who had been Rose's longtime friend, gave a brief description of her life and said a final farewell. He hinted she would be happier in heaven. There was no mention of Ron.

I craved more clarity about the ending of my own relationship. Rose and I experienced a love that ended abruptly. I wanted to compare our stories to better understand why our men could not fully commit to us.

After the priest finished his sermon, I went into a small room adjacent to the chapel. An elderly black man with a cane, sat in the corner. I half-smiled and took a seat not wanting to be noticed.

"You must be Faith," he said.

How do strangers know my name? This was happening more frequently.

When I didn't say anything, he said, "I'll tell you a secret. Rose told me about you the other day when I stopped by for a visit."

"She talked about me? Really? I hardly knew her."

"You made quite an impression, young lady." He smiled.

"How did you know Rose?" I asked.

"Well, this may shock you, but I knew Rose through my brother. My name is Don."

"How did your brother know her?"

"My brother, Ron, dated Rose for a long time." He stopped when he saw the expression on my face.

"Ron is your brother? The man who had an extraordinary love affair with her?"

"Yep, he was my brother. He passed away a few years ago. Rose said it would be okay for me to tell you their story.

She had a feeling she was getting ready to pass on and that you might want to know more." Don shifted in his seat.

"Wow." I couldn't think of anything better to say.

"Their story was tragic. I got to know Ron better through Rose. Even though they had what seemed like a loving relationship, he wasn't able to fully commit to her."

"I see." His story matched what Rose had told me.

"Before Rose met Ron, she didn't want to get married. This changed after she met him. But Ron was never really ready to give her his complete heart. He was too stubborn, and too free spirited, to change his lifestyle for love. You know, he did that once already and when he lost his first wife to cancer, he didn't want to go through that pain again. Can you believe that? It was sad. Rose told me it was a gift to share his life, even if he couldn't provide the kind of love she deserved."

"How long were they together? Was he faithful to her?"

"Oh, they dated casually for about twenty years. It was a long relationship. I do hope he was faithful. I always wondered if he was just too damn scared of commitment."

"Well, it's amazing she stayed with him for all that time."

"Yeah, it was. They were in tune spiritually, emotionally, and physically. I've never myself found that kind of connection with someone. For Ron, it was pretty special."

"Do you know why Rose had her palms face up in her casket? Her hands were like that the other night when we talked."

"You have a lot of questions, don't you?" He chuckled. "It was tragic and unexpected when Ron passed away because of their connection. It was magical. Rose was devastated, as I'm sure you can imagine."

"Yes."

Don nodded. "This is why Rose looked into the magic window: she could sense he was there. She also had dreams where he came to her and apologized for not giving more of himself. After all this time, it was when he died that he finally chose to be fully committed to her." He breathed in a long sigh.

"Rose had a fascination with hands, especially his. In his last breath before he died, Ron told her he would always be holding her hand. Once, she even said she felt his hands in hers and I believed her." Don had a faraway look in his eyes.

"I believe it." I glanced back at her casket. "I love the dress she has on today."

"Well, you'll find this interesting. Rose was not her real name. It was a nickname Ron gave her once they started dating. They said the rose defined their love, so that explains her dress."

"That's beautiful. So, what's her real name?"

"I'm sorry to say, I don't know. Ron never told me, but when they first started dating, he told me that every month for the first six months, he bought her a different colored rose. Each color had a different meaning and Rose was big on meanings. Somehow, the name Rose stuck. She told me she wanted to die to be with him." He wiped a tear from his eye.

"What an extraordinary story. Rose got her wish. I feel better after talking with you. Thank you."

"You're welcome, Faith." Don started to stand up with the help of his cane. "I should get going but it was a pleasure to meet you. I'm glad I could shed light on their love affair and answer some questions for you."

"Me, too. This was unexpected but much appreciated. I feel better that she's in heaven with Ron."

We said goodbye and, as Don started to walk away, he turned around. "By the way, you should have faith that you'll find a connection like theirs. In my lifetime, I've learned it only happens to really special people, and I know you're one special lady."

"Thank you. That's sweet of you to say." I walked away, smiling, knowing there were true lessons in the information I learned. I felt much better knowing that Rose finally got what she wanted.

Chapter 7

Time seemed to pass quickly. Mid-April brought lots of rain. St. Lucille's filled my days and had become a significant part of my life.

One evening after my shift, I tapped on the door to Lance's room and walked in. As expected, Gracie sat next to him while he slept. It had been a few weeks since we last spoke.

When Gracie saw me, her face lit up. She motioned for me to come inside and put a finger to her lips, reminding me to be quiet. Lance's face had more wrinkles than when I last saw him. His bones were visible beneath his thinning skin and he looked much older.

I sat in a chair next to Gracie.

She turned to me and whispered, "It's great to see you. These past two months have taken a toll on Lance. He's been tired a lot and at times, he doesn't even recognize me."

"I'm sorry to hear that. If you'd like to go for a walk sometime, to get away for a while, let me know."

"That's so nice of you. I may take you up on that. My life revolves around him. When I'm at home, my heart is here." She let out a small sigh and returned her gaze to his frail body.

We quietly watched Lance's chest move up and down. After spending so much time around humming respirators, I realized how much I'd taken for granted what a gift it was to breathe.

I stayed with Gracie for an hour, wondering if Lance would wake up so we could all talk. He slept the entire time. Eventually, I told Gracie I'd catch up with her later and left.

Someday, I hope to have a strong love like theirs. I closed my eyes and saw Cole's handsome face.

A few days later, I walked past Lance's room in the evening. Gracie was there, as dedicated to him as always. I stood in the doorway for a long while. Gracie looked frail and her head rested on Lance's hand. I heard a quiet weep and wanted to go over to her, but I didn't want to startle her.

After some time, Gracie looked at me. Her eyes pierced through the darkness, yet her voice was soft and gentle. "Faith, is that you?"

"Yes, it's me. May I come in?"

"Of course. Lance has taken a turn for the worse. I'm really afraid he isn't going to make it," she whimpered.

I walked over and gave her a hug. She fell into my arms like a rag doll. We held each other. She was one of the angels in this place.

When Gracie started to pull back, tears streamed down her face. She dabbed her eyes with a tissue and whispered,

"He won't live much longer. I can't live without him. I just can't."

"Gracie, you've been here night and day. Lance appreciates you so much for it. I know he doesn't want to leave you, but he may have to go sooner than he had wanted to. When he's gone physically, he'll be with you spiritually. I promise you that. I'll take care of you any way I can." I surprised myself with the declaration.

Gracie looked at me again and cried. I could tell she was grateful for what I'd said and maybe even believed it. I walked her home that night, determined to keep my promise.

Morning came quickly and I was running late. My alarm didn't go off. The batteries were dead. I quickly dressed and headed to work.

When I walked into St. Lucille's, people were sniffling, their eyes glued to the ground. Immediately, I knew what had happened. I rushed to Lance's room. His head lay in Gracie's arms. She was crying. My eyes filled with tears. Remembering my promise, I left to find Gayle.

I found her rummaging around in the maintenance closet. "Hi, Gayle."

"Hello, Faith." She glanced at me. "I'm so sorry about Lance. I know you were trying to get to know him. Gracie just adores you."

"How do you do it? How do you hold it together when someone dies?" I sniffled.

"You know what? I'm sad, really, I am, but I've worked here for so many years. It's a natural part of life. People live and then they pass on. Some of them are much happier up there." She pointed to the ceiling.

"I know. Now Gracie will be alone. She came here

every single day for the past few years. She and Lance were so in love."

"They're still in love, Faith. This is what you have to remember. Just because he's gone and we can't see him, doesn't mean he has left Gracie's heart. He'll always be with her."

"Yes, I know." Then I remembered the reason I wanted to talk with Gayle. "I need your help. I know this is short notice, but I think Gracie needs somebody to help her and I said I would be there for her. I'm not sure how that'll go but I want to keep my promise. Is it possible to get a few days off?"

Gayle turned to look at me. "Faith, you are one of the most thoughtful employees here. You really care about these people. It's refreshing to have you work with us. And yes, I know Gracie needs someone to be with her for the next couple of days. But we also need you here. There are so many people whose lives you brighten. I think you should take the next two days off to be with Gracie. Then you can call me. I think she'll be okay by then. If not, we can have one of the other staff members stay with her for a while."

"Thank you so much, Gayle. I really appreciate it."

I thought about everything Gayle said to me. Some residents might be disappointed if they didn't see me for a few days. I popped in on my regulars and explained the situation.

They echoed the same comment. "Take real good care of Gracie and hurry back."

෬ ෩

The next couple of days were difficult and tiring. I provided solace to Gracie and stood by her while she said goodbye to her beloved Lance. It was disquieting staying in their home. Lance's clothes were still in the closet and I pretended not to notice when Gracie held his robe to her face to inhale his scent. Photos of the two of them were propped on every shelf. Gracie sprayed his cologne in the air. I saw sadness in Gracie's eyes and sensed the overwhelming pain in her soul. She often had crying spells. I tried to talk with her, but she didn't hear me nor did she speak to me. Shock and denial struck her hard.

On my last day there, I awoke, walked into the kitchen and made a pot of tea. Gracie strolled into the dining room. When I brought her a cup of tea, she said, "Faith, Lance came to me in my dream last night."

My eyes grew big. "Really? What happened?"

"It seemed so real to me, almost more real than ordinary life. It was as though we were together again. I saw him and he looked just as happy as he was ten years ago. And he was so vibrant and alive!"

"Really?"

She nodded. "He told me how much he still loves me. He knew when I awoke that I would be without him. He said he'll watch over me and he looks forward to the day I can go and be with him. I know it was a dream, a wonderful dream. I believe he is with me, just as you told me the night before he died. Our love continues to bring me great comfort."

I reached for her hand and squeezed it. "I hope we can share more stories like this as they happen." I smiled.

"I know the road ahead will be difficult, but now that I know he's near, I'll talk with him and hope to see him again in my dreams." She seemed to feel better. "As long as I'm here, he's here. So, I think you should go back to work. The residents love and miss you, and they'll be so glad to see you again."

"Do you feel him now?"

"I do, in fact. I'm more in love with him today than I was on our wedding day."

"That's a wonderful gift after these last few sad days." I gave Gracie a long bear hug and said goodbye.

Once home, I crashed.

Chapter 8

The end of May came quickly. One day, Gracie popped into St. Lucille's for a surprise visit. I gave her a hug.

"It's nice to see you too, sweetie," she said, after loosening her hold on me.

"How are you doing? I've missed you," I said.

"I feel better. Every day is a step forward. It's good to see my friends here."

"Have you had any more dreams?" My voice softened.

"Yes and that's one reason I'm here. After I visit with my friends, do you have some free time?" She winked. "I have something to tell you."

Gracie said she wanted to show me a special place in the valley that she and Lance had frequented. We agreed to meet late in the afternoon.

The rest of the day flew by as I visited with the residents. By early evening, my heart thumped with excitement. Gracie was so special to me and I couldn't wait to spend more time with her. I said farewell to the staff and ran home to change.

"Hi, Gracie!" I met her at the start of the trail, close to my house.

She turned and smiled. Her silver hair was in a bun and thin wisps hung over her ears. Her big green eyes were bright and her cheeks glowed. "Hi, Faith!"

"What's going on with you? You look so happy."

"I feel so good. I know my Lance passed but I see him in my dreams and I feel him when I'm awake. It's amazing."

"I want to hear all about it."

As we walked down a hill, she said, "We connected on every level when he was alive."

"Did it come naturally?"

"No, it took a lot of work and patience. I was lucky. Lance's death was the hardest thing in my life, although I felt he had already left a lot earlier than the day he actually died. But you're right: he lives in my heart. Remember when I told you that Lance came to me in my dream and I could feel him the next day? Well, that second night, I dreamed of him again."

"Really?"

Gracie nodded, smiling. "We were together and it was remarkable. I remember every detail about the dream as though I were awake. On the third day, I sensed he was around me. So, I did something I normally wouldn't do. I talked to him. I asked him to do something to let me know that he was here with me."

"And did he?"

"Yes. On that day, I smelled a whiff of his cologne. He was right next to me. Our connection has been strong since the moment we met. I don't want to make you feel squeamish when I tell you this next part. Are you sure you're up for it?"

"Of course. You have to tell me. I want to know."

"Since that night, I've been given this new gift. When I dream, I know I'm dreaming. Have you ever had dreams like that?"

"No." I was feeling envious.

"I asked Lance where he was and he said he was in this beautiful, warm and sunny place. I asked him what he does all day and he told me he thinks about me. He comes to me when I'm awake and when I'm asleep." She glanced over at me and I gestured for her to continue. "Every day we talk and then I see him in my dreams at night. It's as if he never left. We're spiritually in tune."

"I believe you. The kind of love I saw between you two was incredible. I've never been in love like that. You're one very lucky woman." I was jealous.

"It's a remarkable experience."

We reached our destination and sat on a bench. Rocky bluffs dotted the valley and the sky was bathed in orange and red. My eyes watered; it was beautiful.

"Honestly, Faith, this looks like heaven, the way Lance described it to me. Since he died, I come here once a week and look out over the valley. Instantly, I feel a serenity and peacefulness I've only felt with Lance by my side. It's powerful."

"Do you feel him now?" I asked, wondering what it would be like to be that close to someone who had died.

"I feel his presence more when I'm alone."

"I understand. It's a strong connection. I hope one day, I'm as fortunate as the two of you," I said.

She nodded. "Thank you for listening and for still

accepting me. Some people don't believe in stuff like this. I really wanted to tell you."

The glow of the sun was disappearing and the wind started to nip at my skin. The cool breeze curled in the sandy dunes. Glad I'd worn a long-sleeved shirt, I stood up, turned around and headed in the direction of home. Gracie wasn't following me.

I turned around. "Are you okay?"

"I'm fine, but I must tell you one last thing before we leave. This is difficult for me to say, but I promised Lance I would . . ."

It dawned on me that she might be very ill. "It's okay, I'll understand."

I hugged my shivering body and watched Gracie take a deep breath and slowly let it out.

"I apologize if this comes as a shock. I'm not sure how much you remember, but I knew your mother."

My breathing turned shallow. I thought my heart had stopped beating. *What?* I felt paralyzed. *What did she say?*

"Don't say anything. Let me continue. I know this must sound strange, but your mother died in Hill City last year." Gracie stroked my arm.

Her words froze in mid-air. The red-orange sky spun above me. I must've stumbled, because I felt Gracie's hand tightly grip my upper arm.

"Dear, let's sit down. I want to tell you more." She gently led me to another bench.

Everything seemed unreal, almost like a dream. *My mother? Is that what she said, something about knowing Mom?*

My mind flashed to my last memory of her. She gave me a kiss and told me she loved me the night before I left for New York City. Involuntarily, my hand grazed my forehead where she had kissed me.

Gracie's arms circled me as she rocked me back and forth. "Oh, Faith. I didn't mean to upset you. It didn't occur to me that maybe you and your mother . . . Well, never mind. Maybe this would be a better conversation to have at another time, but I did promise Lance I'd tell you tonight. I would feel horrible if I didn't keep my promise."

When I opened my mouth, it was dry. I closed it, licked my lips, and said with a gasp, "Oh, my God! My mom died?"

"I'm so sorry," Gracie said.

"I can't remember her. Why can't I remember?"

Oblivious to my confusion about my memory loss, Gracie said, "Your mother was my best friend. You're just like her, so it's no wonder I get along so well with you. You don't know how happy I was to see you the first time we met. She said you would come back one day, but I wasn't sure. She was really sick during her final years."

My head was spinning.

She looked at me sympathetically and said, "Your mother was a vibrant woman who loved life. When she walked into the room, everyone gravitated to her. She loved you so much. I'm not sure what happened between the two of you, but whatever it was, it didn't affect how she felt about . . ."

"Stop!" I couldn't hear any more. Tears streamed down my face.

"There now, my dear." I heard Gracie say, as though she didn't hear me.

I felt a huge weight of regret.

"Shhhh . . . it's okay." She tried to soothe me. "I

think we should get going. It's getting cold and dark and I'm afraid we won't find our way back. I'll tell you whatever you want to know, but I think I've said enough for tonight."

I wanted to go home.

"Before we go, I want to show you something," Gracie said as she rose to her feet. "It's kind of dark now and it may be hard to see, but do you see that small light over there to the left of the hill, kind of in the valley?"

I tried to squint, wiping my eyes with the sleeve of my shirt. "I think so." Tears blurred my vision.

"Well, that's where your mother is buried. Maybe sometime we can go there together."

I looked again as though it might be the last time I would see it.

I managed to walk home with Gracie. I couldn't say a word even if I wanted to. I needed to be alone and sensed Gracie understood this.

Once home, I headed straight to bed.

It seemed like ages since I was depressed, but now, I felt the sadness resurface. I could hear the pine needles rustle in the wind, a sound I had learned to love. I tried to sleep but I couldn't stop thinking. I had so many questions.

Chapter 9

The alarm buzzed in my ear the next morning. I pushed the snooze button a dozen times before I finally stumbled out of bed. As I scrambled to get out the door, I was overcome with grief. I didn't know if I could handle work right now. I needed time alone to absorb Gracie's revelation. I dialed St. Lucille's number.

"Hello?" Gayle answered.

Caught off guard at how quickly she picked up the phone, I said, "Hi, Gayle, it's me, Faith."

"You sound different. What happened? Are you alright?"

"Well, no, not really. I'm calling in sick today." Without really thinking, the words flew out of my mouth. "Actually, I need to take this week off. I'm really sorry to do this to you on such short notice, but something has come up. I can't say more right now." I was stunned by the idea now brewing in my mind.

Gayle said she understood.

I had never called in sick. As difficult as it was, I needed answers.

I called Terese and left a message. "Hey, Terese. Something's come up. I'll be in New York City for a few days. I need to talk with you."

I booked an early evening flight. I packed only the necessities: underwear, a couple pairs of jeans, some shirts, and my toothbrush. I called a cab for a ride to the airport and, before I knew it, I was at the terminal.

My mind was foggy as I boarded the plane. Once I was in my seat, I let out a big sigh and closed my eyes. The plane taxied onto the runway and rose into the air.

The pilot startled me awake. "Folks, we will be arriving in New York City in ten minutes. The weather is seventy degrees and cloudy. The local time is 9:30 p.m.. Thank you for flying with us and enjoy your stay."

I glanced out the window. The city was lit up beneath us. Surprisingly, I hadn't missed it. Compared to Hill City, the Big Apple felt too congested.

When we landed, I grabbed my carry-on and walked outside into the warm air, typical for late May. At a crosswalk, a familiar voice called out "Faith! Faith!"

Terese was running toward me, waving her arms and jumping up and down.

"Oh, my God! How did you know I was here?" I wasn't sure whether to laugh or cry. We hugged.

"After you left that message, I went online and found your flight."

Being with my best friend lifted my mood. Terese unlocked the doors and we got into her Jeep. "Can I crash at your place?"

"Yes, of course. I'm thrilled you're here. What's going on that's so urgent?"

The weight of my emotions pressed into my heart and my eyes watered. "Oh, God. Well . . ."

"Let's talk about it a little later. You said you were staying a few days, right? We have time. What I really want to know is how you've been. I've missed talking with you and I'm sorry I haven't called. I've been so busy with work."

I sighed with relief. I wasn't ready to talk about Mom yet. Relaxing into the car seat, I said, "It's okay. I've been really busy, too. I love my life."

"I'm so happy for you. You deserve to feel good again." She turned the car into an underground garage beneath an apartment complex I didn't recognize.

"This place looks different. Did you move?"

"Yes, I did. It feels like ages since we've seen each other. I live in a penthouse now."

"Oh, how snazzy."

We rode the elevator to the tenth floor. When the door opened, spread before us was an ultra-modern, expensive apartment. Pendant lights hung from the ceiling in the kitchen. There was a stainless-steel refrigerator and dishwasher. The spacious living room held a rich, brown leather couch and armchair, and a large TV. A long rectangular balcony behind floor-to-ceiling sliding glass doors revealed a view overlooking the city.

"Wow, this is really nice. Show me the rest."

"Of course, Ms. Faith," Terese joked as we walked further into her home. "Here's my bedroom with a master bathroom. As you can see, there's a Jacuzzi, too."

"This is so romantic. I love the red candles."

"This is where you'll stay." She took me to my bedroom

that had an adjacent private bathroom with a Jacuzzi. "You'll have to ignore my constant enthusiasm. I'm still so thrilled this place is mine."

"I totally understand. This is really great. My own bathroom. I can't wait to use it." We both giggled.

"I'm sure you must be tired. Would you like to take a little nap or freshen up for an hour? There is fresh fruit on the dresser in case you're hungry."

"Thank you, I'd like that." The quiet time was inviting. I unpacked, ate an apple and took a long bath. After I dried off, I squeezed lemon scented lotion into my palms, and massaged it over my pelvis, stomach and chest, finishing at my neck. I put on my pajamas, crawled into bed and closed my eyes, enjoying the tingly and invigorating feeling created by the cream. A surprising sense of comfort soothed my mind and stilled my thoughts. I was able to get some sleep, finally.

When I awoke, it took me a minute to remember where I was. I got up and slipped into the robe I found hanging in the guest bedroom closet. I walked into the living room, and saw my best friend going over some paperwork.

"What time is it?" It was still dark outside.

"Oh, hey!" Terese looked up. "It's eleven thirty, but I decided to let you sleep."

"That was so nice of you. I slept soundly, surprisingly. The noisy traffic drowned out my thoughts."

"Oh, I didn't think of the noise. Did it bother you? I forgot to close the windows."

"No, I meant the noise was a good thing. Don't worry about it. Actually, I'm kind of hungry now."

"Yeah. I think we should order in. Vietnamese?" She picked up the phone to place the order.

"That sounds perfect. Thank you." My stomach growled, even though it was nearly twelve in the morning.

I ordered spring rolls and chicken breasts sautéed in ginger. Terese ordered crispy duck with sweet and sour sauce. They promised to deliver our food in just twenty minutes.

"It's great to see you and spend time together," I said.

When our food came, we sat on her balcony and ate by candle-light. I couldn't remember the last time I had eaten Vietnamese food.

"Oh, man, this is delicious," I said between mouthfuls. The skyline was beautiful, even in the inner city.

"I don't want to rush you to talk about whatever you came here to talk about, but I want you to know that whenever you want to bring it up, I'm here to listen."

"I really appreciate that. Maybe we can talk about it tomorrow." *How much should I tell her? What will she think of my lack of memory? Will she have the answers I've come to find?*

∽ ∽

The next day, I woke up at 9:00 a.m. and drank a glass of orange juice. The apartment was quiet. *Terese must still be asleep.*

I went back to bed. I wanted to tell Terese everything that had happened with Gracie, including all the events that led up to the shocking news about Mom. My eyelids grew heavy when I thought about it all over again.

I awoke the second time at 11:00 a.m., and dragged myself out of bed and to the living room where I found a note from Terese.

Good morning, sleepyhead! I have a surprise for you. Dress comfortably, and I'll pick you up at 1:00 p.m.. Love, T.

Finding Faith

I smiled at Terese's sweetness, wondering what she had up her sleeve. Then I showered, dressed, and ate some cereal and a banana.

Around 12:45 p.m., the phone rang. I let it ring until I heard Terese's voice on the answering machine. She asked me to pick up the phone and instructed me to be in the lobby in fifteen minutes.

When I got downstairs, I saw Terese waiting outside in her Jeep. I went to meet her.

Terese rolled down her window. "Well, look who finally woke up," she teased.

"I actually got up earlier and thought you were sleeping, so I went back to bed. Where are we going?" I asked as I hopped into her car.

"I'm treating us to a spa day. I've heard great things about this place and I've been looking for an opportunity to go. I've never been to a spa before. Can you believe it?"

"Wow. Neither have I. This sounds wonderful, thank you so much. How about I treat you to dinner afterwards?"

"I'd love that."

The rustic looking spa was nestled in a cute neighborhood on a dead-end street in Queens, in a calm and quiet part of the city. Inside, there were maroon walls and beige candles in every corner. We both had the same kind of wow expression. I anticipated our moments of massage bliss.

A young receptionist greeted us and offered warm green tea. Soon we followed an older woman to a dimly lit room. Before she left, she instructed us to undress and lay down on the massage tables.

A few minutes later, two female masseuses walked in. "Hi, ladies. Feel free to close your eyes and rest."

"Okay," we both echoed.

It seemed like hours later when we awoke. I thought I'd feel groggy, but I felt refreshed and awake. We slowly sat up, walked into private rooms to shower and change back into our clothes.

Terese met me afterwards, and said, "That was heavenly."

The women returned and told us where to go for a manicure and pedicure.

"There's more?"

"Of course, we're at a spa," Terese teased.

Unfortunately, they separated us for the next part, but that was okay. I was so relaxed and savored that feeling.

∽ ∾

After our zen experience, Terese drove us to a small Japanese barbecue restaurant. They seated us toward the back. A mini grill was in the middle of the table.

"What's the grill for? Warmth?" I'd never eaten in a Japanese restaurant.

"No, silly, we're going to cook on it," Teresa laughed.

"Way cool." I bubbled with enthusiasm. Once we ordered, I took a deep breath. "I think now is a good time to tell you about what happened in Hill City."

I told her about Gracie, how we met and became good friends. Then our food arrived.

"Let's stop for a minute so I can explain how to cook your food." Terese showed me how to prepare my food.

When it was finished cooking, I tasted my first barbecue, Japanese style. "This is delicious." I took a few more bites of grilled chicken.

"Yes, it is. Continue with your story."

"So, after her husband Lance died, Gracie wanted to talk with me about something."

"Right, go on."

"Gracie said she knew my mom and that my mom passed away *last year*."

"Wow, I'm so sorry to hear that. How do you feel?"

"I'm so so sad, and I'm still in shock. The strange thing is I don't remember much about my mom. I didn't even know she was sick and that she passed away, otherwise, I would've been with her. When I went to Hill City, you know, it seemed so familiar, but I wasn't sure why. I met people who told me I looked familiar. Now I know the reason. What happened to me, Terese? I figured you'd know something." I felt tears collect in my eyes.

"Well . . . I do know some of what happened. Don't be mad but this is the reason I bought you a ticket to Hill City so you could learn about your past," Terese slowly began.

At that moment, the waitress came to ask us if we wanted anything else.

"Let's get some dessert and plum wine. By the time we dive into this topic, we'll need to be a little more relaxed," Terese smiled.

When the waitress left, Terese continued, "I know you and your mom were really close. When you first moved here, you always talked about her, and stayed in contact with her. Then when *Daniel* moved in with you, things changed." Terese's body tensed.

"What do you mean, things changed?"

"I don't think Daniel wanted you to have contact with your mom. He likely felt threatened by her and thought she would knock some sense into you and you would leave him."

"Really? Why can't I remember that?"

"Well, I only know bits and pieces," Terese said. The mango sherbet arrived with our plum wine. Terese made a toast, "To our friendship and finding answers."

"I'm not hungry anymore." I pushed the sherbet in Terese's direction and gulped down half of my wine.

Terese saw the expression on my face and continued with the story. "Here's what I know. One day when I got home from work, I got a call from an emergency room doctor stating that you had been admitted. You had given them my contact information. I had no idea what happened but was told to come quickly. I was really scared."

"I was in the hospital? When did that happen?" I drank all of my wine and flagged down the waitress to order another glass.

"You were lying in bed half-dazed and you looked really, really bad. This happened six months after you moved in together."

"What do you mean, I looked really bad? What happened to me?"

"I'm not sure, but the doctor said that according to Daniel, you fell down a flight of stairs, which made no sense since there were only three stairs outside your apartment complex. You had black and blue marks on your face and your head was wrapped in bandages. The doctor said you were struggling in and out of consciousness." Her eyes filled with tears.

"Oh, my God! Really?"

"Back then, I didn't believe Daniel's story and to this day, I still don't." She carefully wiped a tear from her eye. I could sense how much anger she probably still had toward him.

"What do you mean?"

"I always wondered if he had something to do with your fall," she admitted.

"Are you serious?" *What's she implying?*

"He was super possessive. He moved in with you quickly, and didn't want you to talk with your mom." She crumpled her napkin tightly between her fingers.

Horror spread through me like ice. My body broke into a sweat. My legs shook involuntarily under the table.

"I'm pretty sure Daniel abused you in some way and then lied and said you fell down steps. Even the doctor seemed suspicious about how you had those injuries from falling down only three stairs." Terese looked at me with conviction in her eyes.

I cleared my throat. "Abused me? I don't remember anything like that happening. What injuries are you talking about?"

"I screamed and begged the doctor to tell me what happened. In an effort to keep me quiet, he told me that you might not be able to remember things that happened prior to or after the fall. He said you had a form of retrograde amnesia, and that it could take you a while to recover from the fall, and it did. It took you a few months to get better. Because you never mentioned the fall, being in the hospital or your mom, I thought you regained your memory. But now, I don't think so."

"I think you're right. I don't remember much. This is so scary and sad."

"This is the main reason Daniel wasn't good for you. This is why I showed little sympathy when he left you."

I vaguely remembered a few comments Terese had made during my relationship with Daniel, when she said that he wasn't good for me. Once she even said I was better off without him. Her plea to get me away from him was starting to make sense now. Suddenly, I felt like an idiot for staying with Daniel.

"What the hell is retrograde amnesia? What else did the doctor say about my memory?"

"That's all he told me. He said this was something that would either gradually get better over time or simply not improve. I can't remember much more than that. I'm really sorry. He also said, it may take a lifetime for you to remember certain people and things."

I sat there stunned, unable to figure out how to process not only the brain injury but also my condition today. My mind spun with questions and confusion.

I didn't want to believe it, but this explained why I simply forgot about Mom. I was surprised I wasn't more upset, but it was difficult to be mad when I had little recollection.

I sipped more wine to numb my senses. "Did my mom ever know what happened to me?"

"Your mom never knew what happened to you. I blame myself for that. She also called occasionally but told me to promise not to say anything to you. She was losing her memory and didn't want to hurt you if she couldn't remember you. She had happy memories of the two of you and chose to hang onto those memories. I thought you might have gotten in touch with her after your time in the hospital. . ."

"This had nothing to do with you, plus you've always been a good friend. I'm not mad at you, and I don't blame you. The damned thing was that I trusted Daniel."

Terese added, "Don't blame yourself for trusting him. That's what couples do when they're in love."

Finding Faith

"He was a jerk and a fake and deceitful ass!"

"Yeah, he was. You know, sometimes mothers have an intuition about their daughters, and unfortunately, in this case, she was right. I think you could learn more about your relationship with your mother from Gracie."

Still in shock, I wondered aloud. "Even though I like learning about my mom, it's too late. She died and—"

Terese interrupted, "That's not true. This is a new beginning in your relationship with your mom. When you forgot her, you were lost for a couple years. You didn't know about her because you couldn't remember, but she'll always be with you in your heart. Just because she isn't here physically doesn't mean she isn't with you spiritually."

That sounded familiar.

Terese continued to stroke my arm, but all I wanted to do was jump out of my seat and bust out the door. I calmed down enough to finish my wine.

I excused myself and went to the bathroom to splash water on my face. I was emotional after learning this information. When I exited the restroom, I bumped into someone.

"Pardon me," I said.

"Excuse me," a masculine voice said, in a huff.

When I looked up, Cole was standing in front of me. *What the—?*

"Why, hello, Allie. Fancy meeting you here." He smiled mischievously.

"Look who's here." I half-smiled. I was at a loss for words. *When did I see him last? Was it Valentine's Day?*

"It's nice to see you, too," Cole said. "I'm actually just leaving. I was having dinner with a friend."

"That's ironic. Me too. Would you like to meet her?" I asked.

"Actually, I'm on my way out. My friend is waiting. Maybe next time?"

I nodded. *Will I see him again?*

"Actually, my friend can wait a few minutes." Cole grabbed my hand and led me down the corridor to the back of the restaurant.

"Where are—?" I tried to ask.

Once we went through the back door, Cole leaned me up against the back of the restaurant. He ran his fingers gently over my arms and my neck. Then, he cupped my face in his hands.

My heart raced. I was captivated by this man. He was so handsome and so seductive. Just then, I realized how much I had missed kissing him.

As if reading my mind, Cole kissed me. His hands glided over my pelvis and cupped each breast.

When I came up for air, I exhaled, "I've missed you."

His pelvis laid into my body pinning me to the wall of the restaurant. He started breathing heavily.

"I've missed you too," Cole huffed. "My friend is waiting, and I don't have time to rock your world today."

"When will I see you again?"

"I don't know." Cole continued to kiss me softly at first, and then harder and harder. "I can't get enough of you."

Cole stepped back and straightened his shirt, and ran his hand over his pelvis. "Damn, see what you do to me?"

I looked down and saw a pulsating bulge. I tingled inside.

Cole kissed me again. Then, he grabbed the door and held it open for me. We said goodbye, and I went back into the bathroom.

Did that really happen? In the mirror, my hair was messy, but I was glowing.

When I got back to the table, Terese wasn't there, so I sat down, hoping she would reappear.

A while later, Terese walked to the table and sat down.

"Where did you go?" I asked, in a calm voice.

"Oh, I saw a friend and we talked for a few minutes outside," she said.

"That's nice," I said.

"Do you feel better?" she asked.

"Much better. Thanks for everything today. Besides finding out about the trauma in my life, it was nice being with you." Little did she know about my passionate kiss with Cole only moments ago.

Chapter 10

I boarded a plane back to Arizona at the end of my stay. Every time I thought about kissing Cole, I felt tingly sensations in my gut.

༄ ༄

I was eager to visit the cemetery where Mom was buried before I returned to work. I arrived back in town early in the evening and called Gracie.

"Faith! Are you back in town? Are you alright? I've been worried about you."

"I was upset because I didn't understand what you told me about my mom. I needed to talk with my best friend and that was the reason for my visit to New York City. I feel better now. I want to tell you all about my time away. Come out with me tonight. We can go to Betty's, my treat."

When I arrived at her house, I saw her peeking out from her window. She smiled, waved, and walked down the front steps to greet me.

"Welcome back, my dear. I'm so happy to see you and

I want to hear about everything. I remember your mother saying you had a girlfriend in New York City. I know she felt better knowing you had a close friend nearby, especially when she couldn't connect with you," she said, rubbing my back.

"That's nice. How's everyone at St. Lucille's? I've missed them. Have you been back there to visit?"

"Yes, they are all doing the same, really. The residents ask about you every day and they look forward to seeing you again."

"And how are you?" We looped arms and walked down the road.

"Oh dear, I feel better now that you're back in town. I missed our walks and wanted to talk with you again about the other night." She glanced up at me.

"I missed you too. You know what? What you told me about my mom was such a precious gift. I just needed some answers."

"Did you get the answers you were looking for?"

"Yes and more." We approached the restaurant.

At Betty's, we sat next to the window. I ordered a grilled cheese sandwich and a butterscotch malt. Gracie ordered a salad and vanilla malt. When the server left, I didn't stall with small talk.

"First of all, thank you for telling me about my mom. I thought you were going to tell me something else that night."

"Oh, I see." Gracie looked apologetic. "What did you think I was going to say?"

The food came quickly. I wasn't completely sure I wanted to tell her. "I thought you were going to tell me you were very sick."

"Oh, I didn't mean to worry you. Just so you know, I'm as healthy as can be." She smiled.

"Good."

I was hoping Gracie would be around for a long time. I sipped my malt and explained why I had moved to New York City and how, soon after I moved, everything started to snowball at a very fast pace with Daniel.

"Terese believed my mom had an intuition that Daniel wasn't a good guy. Do you know if my mom was worried about me? And, is there a reason you didn't tell me all of this earlier?"

"I know she was worried about you because soon after you moved you lived with someone you knew so little about. Your mom was a wise woman and she had a bad feeling about all of it."

"Okay," I said, letting this information sink in.

"And as for the reasons why I didn't say anything sooner, well, we met when Lance's health was deteriorating and I wanted to get to know you a little better before I told you about your mother." Gracie dabbed her mouth with a napkin.

"Okay." I still didn't get it, but I didn't want to argue with her.

"Terese alluded to Daniel being very controlling, and we think he felt threatened by the closeness that I had with my mom. You know, Daniel was quite the charmer. He was also very handsome. I'd never been with a man like him before, so at the time, I felt pretty lucky. Terese also told me there was an accident that resulted in me losing my memory," I shared.

Gracie stopped chewing. "What do you mean by losing your memory?"

"I don't remember whole slices of my life. I ended up in the hospital one day and . . ."

"Oh my goodness! What happened?"

"Daniel told the doctor I had fallen down the front stairs at our home. Terese said my eyes and forehead were black and blue and I had bandages wrapped around my head. The doctor said I had a brain injury. Terese thinks Daniel hurt me." I paused to sip my malt.

Gracie looked at me, wide-eyed.

"The doctor told Terese I may not regain my memory." Saying it aloud made me realize how unreal it still seemed.

"Oh my, that must be so frightening!" Gracie sighed as her eyes searched mine for answers. "It sounds like he had some issues. I can't believe that happened to you, and I'm really sorry. Your mom was right. Had she known you were hurt, she would've been on the next plane out to see you."

"I feel so sad that I stopped communicating with her." I lowered my eyes in shame and guilt.

"Your mom wondered about you, but she knew you had Terese and so she worried a little less. I knew her for the last two years of her life and then she passed away peacefully in her sleep. She loved you very much, and she knew you would return to Hill City one day," she said, with a reassuring smile.

I was too caught up in the story and continued talking, oblivious to what Gracie had just said. "This is all my fault. It didn't occur to me to think about Mom. What had been so important in my life, to put my relationship with her on hold? I know I was hurt. I feel much sadness about all this."

"Dear, it's not your fault. But I'm relieved you finally

found out what happened." She reached across the table, took my hand and squeezed it.

"I really want to go see Mom. If you give me directions, I think I can find her in the cemetery. There are so many things I want to tell her. Plus, when I try to remember her, I feel warm. Does that sound strange?"

"No, because I feel Lance, as you know," she reminded me as she finished her salad.

Gracie pulled out a piece of paper and a pen from her purse. "Here, let me draw you a map of how to get to the cemetery." She gave the map to me.

I smiled. "Thank you." I stuffed it into my pocket. "I really want you to tell me all about my mom. I want you to be my link to her. I want to dream about her. Can we meet for walks and talk about her?"

"Of course we can. I promised your mom before she died, that if I was fortunate enough to meet you, I would look after you." Her eyes sparkled.

"That's so nice." I smiled, and paid for our meal. "Thank you again for all of your kindness. I missed you when I was away and I'm glad to be home again. Now I know why it seemed so difficult to come back here. I always had a feeling about this place."

On our walk home, I said, "The strange thing is I don't even remember much about Hill City. For a long time, I really haven't felt like myself. That scares me." *Am I still experiencing the memory loss?*

"Well, who knows what really happened to you. You may want to go to a doctor in the area and have it checked out so you know for sure. I know a good doctor twenty minutes outside of town."

I was quiet. I had so many questions.

"Oh boy, there's so much to tell you about your mom. If it's any comfort, you didn't grow up in Hill City."

Chapter 11

The next morning, I felt an overwhelming need to visit Mom. I had also forgotten some of the details from my conversation with Gracie, so I decided to visit her first.

Just as I was about to knock on her door, she opened it. "Hello, Faith. What a nice surprise."

"Hi, Gracie," I smiled.

"Do come in. I've put on some tea. It should be ready soon." She shuffled into the kitchen.

"I'm sorry for stopping by unannounced like this. Could we talk for a bit? That is, if I didn't catch you at a bad time." I followed her into the kitchen.

"Oh no, this is a perfect time. I was just going to have tea and would enjoy the company, especially yours." She poured us a cup.

I looked around. "Your place seems brighter. Did you change it?"

"I opened things up a little. I figured one of the ways

to let in Lance was to bring in more sunlight." She winked.

We sat on the couch.

"So, what would you like to talk about?"

"I've been trying to remember what you said just before we left each other."

"Yes, let me think . . . Oh, sure. I said you didn't grow up in Hill City. Was that it?" She sipped her drink.

"That's it. What did you mean?"

"You and your mom lived in Philadelphia before coming to Hill City. Your mother traveled to Hill City and loved the area, so she chose to move here before you left for New York City."

"Life is a puzzle. I wonder what she loved about Hill City." My eyes were glued to the hills outside Gracie's living room window.

"Your mother loved to garden. She loved to go for walks in the valley, like you do. One of her favorite sounds was the wind in the desert sand. She loved the sunsets, full moons, and the heat. She adored people, which may be why she wanted to stay at St. Lucille's until she died."

"She was at St. Lucille's?" Dumbfounded, I finally knew why my intuition had led me to work there. "Wow. So, did anyone there know Mom, like Gayle or any of the residents?"

"Yes, Gayle knew of your mother and some of the residents may remember her, too. As you know, a few of them suffer from memory loss."

I recalled some of the things people around town had said to me when I first arrived in Hill City, including the way people looked at me.

"I wonder why Gayle never said anything to me?"

"Well, dear, maybe she's waiting for you to bring it up. I'm not sure. You can ask her, especially now that you know more of your story." She folded her hands in her lap.

"Ok, so, what else can you tell me?"

"You remind me of her. You have her beauty and her quiet spirit. Like her, everyone adores you." Gracie looked deep into my eyes. "She was kind and thoughtful, a dear friend. I miss her every day."

The next day I awoke to a ray of sun streaming in through the window. I squinted as the light bounced in slow motion on my bed. The sun and I are like lovers. When I closed my eyes, I heard the wind stir up the sand and songs of nearby birds. I loved my peaceful sanctuary.

I dressed, ate an apple, grabbed the map Gracie made for me, tied my hair in a bun and headed outside for a light jog. I was excited and nervous about finding my way to the cemetery. I turned on my iPod and started with a casual run. Songs uplifted my mood.

It was a hot, dry day in June. Glancing at my watch, I saw how quickly time flew. Between the music and admiring the scenery, thirty minutes had passed. There was a resting spot under a tall juniper tree. I stopped to catch my breath, take a sip of water and look at the map in the shade. I paced, hoping my heart rate would drop.

Once I had cooled down, I leaned against a wall that overlooked a tall, bronze rock formation and I tuned into my thoughts. *What would I say to Mom?* It seemed odd to think about talking to a stone anchored in the ground, but that was my only way to connect with her.

Finding Faith

The rest of the trail was curvy and hilly. My heart rate raced back up as I ran. What I would tell Mom faded when the music played. Some of the songs beckoned for me to run faster and others slowed me down. I wanted to sing along but I was afraid I'd run out of breath.

When I reached the cemetery, towering pine trees smelled like past Christmases. To my surprise, there was some green grass and a mix of wild sedum covering the ground. *Should I have brought flowers?*

The granite headstones looked majestic, glistening in the bright sunlight. I walked around and read the writing on the stones. They each detailed something special about those who had passed.

I didn't know where Mom was buried and there were about a hundred stones in the cemetery. Had I not seen another family there, I would've felt spooked. I walked down each aisle looking for Carolina Neely.

By the fourth row, I was tired. I stopped and looked around. *If I were Mom, where would I want to be buried?*

I remembered Gracie said Mom loved nature. I turned from right to left and saw many stones close together. Since she was never married, I looked for a lone gravesite. Just before completing the full circle, I spotted a stone off to the side near a few tall pine trees, and walked over to it.

This oasis was overflowing with white and yellow daisies, and knee-high, wild grasses. I didn't know plants like these could grow in the desert. When the wind blew, it gave me goosebumps.

In front of me stood a stone that read:

In loving memory of Carolina Neely - Loving Mother and Friend.

The stone was inlaid with green, purple, yellow, blue and red glass. A vase filled with fresh pansies sat in front of her grave. *Who put these here?*

I knelt down on the patch of mossy grass facing the granite marker. I touched it, and felt something tingly on my hand. Quickly, I pulled my hand away. I studied the stone. Finally, after a few moments of awkward silence, I talked to her.

"Hi, Mom." I glanced around to make sure no one saw or heard me. I felt a bit weird talking to a stone. "It's me, Faith. Your daughter." I paused, out of habit, waiting for her to speak.

"You must be surprised to see me in Hill City. I've been waiting a long time to talk to you." I felt calm. It was mid-afternoon and given that I had a few more hours of daylight, I wasn't confident I could fill it up with words.

"I don't have much time today. So much has happened that I want to explain. But for now, I want to sit and be close to you. I hope you know I love you. I just learned that I missed the last years of your life."

I licked my lips. "Gosh, it's so hot today. I feel horrible about how things progressed after I moved to New York City. Things happened that were out of my control. I can explain more later. I feel terrible that I didn't get to talk with you."

The hot sun warmed my forehead, soothing my nerves.

"I'm friends with one of your best friends, Gracie, who told me about you. She's wonderful," I said.

The breeze shifted directions. Pine needles rustled in the trees. The flowers bent in the wind.

It was comforting to sit next to Mom. I lay down,

put my right hand against her headstone, and closed my eyes.

I awoke an hour later feeling refreshed, glad to have experienced some solitude. "Mom, I need to get going before it gets dark. I love and miss you."

A lump lodged in my throat. Tears stung my eyes.

"This is so hard. I hate leaving you, but I'll be back. I promise. I wish you could give me a sign to let me know you can hear me."

I sat for a few more moments not wanting to leave, waiting for a sign. After I wiped my eyes, I stood up. I had a strange urge to give her a kiss, so I bent down until my lips reached the stone and kissed it. Feeling that energy again, I knew I had to talk with Gracie about it. When I looked up, I saw a deer. I gasped. This was the first wild animal I'd seen since I moved here.

I remembered my wish from moments ago and whispered, "Thank you, Mom."

I watched the deer, wondering if it saw me. Slowly, it walked in my direction until we were only ten feet apart. She was so graceful as she stared at me for a few seconds.

Mom? I felt that warm and tingling feeling again, stronger than before.

The wind started to pick up. "Goodbye Mom, I'll be back."

I walked out of the cemetery. When I turned around for a last look, the deer was gone.

Chapter 12

At home, I sat down on the couch and gazed out the big window. The sunset colored the sky with soft red, orange, and yellow hues. I looked in the direction of the cemetery. I couldn't see it, but when I closed my eyes, I was there.

After dinner, I got ready for bed. Between the run and spending time with Mom, I was drained physically and emotionally. I reached for the phone and called St. Lucille's. If I was lucky, maybe they would let me have another day off.

"Hello, St. Lucille's, may I help you?" the man asked on the other end. His attractive voice sounded familiar.

"Yes, this is Faith."

"Are you an employee, family member, or volunteer?"

"I'm an employee. I've been gone for the past week. Is Gayle around?"

"Oh, hi, Faith! I didn't recognize your voice. This

is Leo. Gayle is out today, but she scheduled you to work on Thursday. She figured you might need a few days off before getting back into the swing of things. Will that work for you?"

His sweet voice sent shivers up my spine. It would be weird to fall for a guy at work.

"That sounds really good." I put the phone down. I was eager to see Leo again and thrilled to have a few more days to myself. I went to bed and fell asleep.

The next morning, a warm feeling spread through my body, as I thought about my visit with Mom. I got out of bed and took a shower. My thoughts drifted back to Leo. Something seemed vaguely familiar about him. These memory lapses were becoming more common and more annoying.

I got dressed, ate breakfast, and called Gracie. We met at our usual spot. It was a warm day.

"Hi, Gracie." It was good to see her again.

"Hi, Faith."

We hugged and rocked from side to side, laughing. When we started walking, I told her about my visit to the cemetery.

Gracie asked, "Did you find the place all right? How was it to be there?"

I said I was nervous and excited to see Mom. I told her the map she made led me to the cemetery but I had a hard time finding Mom's grave.

"I'm sorry. I should've told you where it was."

"I finally found her. It was emotional to be there."

"I know. It's difficult to be at someone's gravesite. But she's with you, you know, spiritually." Gracie reached for my hand offering me comfort.

"Before I had to go home, I kissed her stone, and felt a warm and tingly feeling. I told Mom to send me a sign that she was okay. All of a sudden, I saw a deer. It stopped ten feet in front of me."

"What an incredible story."

"So, what do you think?" I was eager to hear Gracie's opinion.

"When I went to see your mom for the first time, after she had passed, I felt a similar feeling. Then when Lance died, I felt that same thing again. After he died, a friend in Minnesota sent me a book about grief. It talks about loss and what happens when people we love die. It says their spirits are near us and these feelings may be their souls trying to communicate with us. Many people can't feel what we feel. It only happens to the lucky ones."

I smiled, hoping that Mom was with us.

We settled on a bench, overlooking the Arizona landscape and talked for a couple of hours. I learned what a remarkable woman my mother was.

When we headed home, Gracie smiled. "I can't remember all your mom said about you, but I'm sure bits and pieces will pop up from time to time."

I looped my arm in Gracie's arm and said, "Tell me something else. You said she spent her last years at St. Lucille's . . ."

"Yes. Gayle made a comment when you got hired. She was tickled pink to have you on staff."

"Cool. What else can you tell me about Mom?" I tried to sound strong.

"Before she was admitted to the nursing home, she cooked regularly and tended to her garden. We took

Finding Faith

long walks into the valley, quite like you and I do. A part of me feels she came back ever since you set foot in Hill City. You've been such a blessing." She waited for my reaction.

"I don't know what to say. Thank you, I guess? Tell me more."

"One day, when she was walking down her back steps to meet me, she fell down. Had I not been just around the corner, bless the Lord, I'm not sure what would've happened."

I gasped, picturing Mom falling down stairs and lying on the ground.

"When I approached the house, I saw her lying there, unresponsive. A hospital is thirty minutes from here, so that would've taken too long. Since my Lance was at St. Lucille's, I called Gayle. We managed to get her into a van and to St. Lucille's. When we got there, your mom was still unconscious and we were all very worried. The staff at St. Lucille's thought she must've had some sort of stroke before the fall. The doctor from the hospital met us there. He confirmed she had suffered a stroke and a concussion. Carolina was unconscious for a couple of days. But on the third day, she was awake. She hadn't recalled how she'd fallen, but she knew who she was and, oddly enough, she remembered you. Most of her other memories were gone."

"Her story mirrors mine a little, don't you think? Then what happened?"

Gracie nodded. "Your mom was admitted to St. Lucille's and then, over the next few months, she became more forgetful. Each day was different. But she never complained, at least not when I was there. It was convenient for me because when I went to see my Lance, I also stopped by to see your mother. We used to see each other daily then."

I nodded. Mom was surrounded by people who cared about her and it made me feel a little better. I wiped a tear from my eye.

Gracie continued, "I remember this next part so well. It was the last night I stopped in to wish your mom a good night's rest when she told me to stay. She asked me to promise to tell you, if we ever met, how much she loved you. She also said I was her best friend. When I realized the reason she was telling me this, I cried because I knew she was ready to pass on. She died in her sleep later that night."

I hugged Gracie and between sobs, whispered, "Thank you for giving me this incredible gift of bringing Mom back into my life. I know it must be hard to tell me about her, but I appreciate it so much."

"I just fulfilled my promise to your mom," she said, hugging me back.

The next day, I awoke early. I only had two more days off and I wanted to see Mom again. I ate breakfast, grabbed my water bottle and ran towards the direction of the cemetery.

The sun was shining, slowly warming the air. The sky was pale blue. Shades of brown bathed the desert. Colorful wildflowers and cacti lined the path.

Halfway to the cemetery, I stopped to sip some water. I looked at the magical wonderland that lay before me and it was clear why Mom wanted to be buried here. I closed my eyes and let the heat seep into me.

Ten minutes passed. Rejuvenated, I ran. The path wound through the hills and valley.

After a while, I saw families talking and laughing with their loved ones. It hadn't dawned on me that this was a place of such joy. I watched them for a while as I caught my breath.

When I looked in Mom's direction, I saw a shadow. I rubbed my eyes and looked again. The shadow was gone.

At Mom's gravesite, there was a fresh bouquet of white lilies. These were different from the pansies that were here the other day. I still had no idea who had put them here.

The grassy area was moist from the early dew. I lay on my back while I looked up at the sky. The wet grass felt good after my hot run.

Awhile later, I sat up. "Hey, Mom, I'm back. I just love this place."

Beyond the graveyard and off into the horizon, colorful layered canyons surrounded us. A Northern Cardinal flew overhead. Prairie dogs ran around only a few feet away. This was truly God's Country.

"I haven't rehearsed anything for today, but I'll start from when I lived in New York City. Hopefully, you'll be able to understand what happened to me." I told Mom everything I had learned from Gracie and Terese.

"I'm sure you beckoned me back to Hill City, especially in light of what I now know about what happened to you." I felt a fountain of pain inside.

I looked over at the stone hoping I would feel a glimpse of her, but all I felt was a slight breeze.

"Gracie is such a Godsend. Her husband died recently and despite her loss, she's been an inspiration for me during this time of rediscovering you. She's the only close friend I have here. I don't remember Hill City, but I'm glad I came back."

I hugged her stone and that warm, tingly feeling permeated throughout my body. I whispered, "I feel you."

I realized Mom had helped me feel and remember again and that was about the best gift a mother could give her daughter.

∽ ∾

The next day, I managed to sleep in, fully aware this was my last day off before I headed back to work. I lay in bed and reflected on my whirlwind adventure. My past was beginning to align with my present. This balance felt good.

In the shower, I closed my eyes. Droplets of water coated my body. I reached for the lemon-scented soap and lathered my arms and legs going very slowly over my curves. I thought about Cole and our deep kiss outside the restaurant in New York City. I was surprised at how sexy I felt. I put my head under the shower and let the water flow over my body.

Soon, I felt suffocated, as though I had been in a hot sauna too long, so I got out, wrapped myself in a cool towel, and smelled the sweet aroma on my skin. I dried off and stood in front of the mirror. Surrendering the towel from my arms, it fell to the floor. My gaze steadied on my wet hair as it hung down. It felt smooth as I raked my hand through it. Then, I looked into my eyes, in an attempt to see my soul.

∽ ∾

The next day, I awoke early enough to eat breakfast on the porch. The sky widened with shades of blue, and the sunlight reached across the sky and stretched above the canyons. It was 8:00 a.m. and I had to be at work soon.

While I sipped hot tea and ate a bowl of cold cereal, a deer slowly made her way into my view. *Mom?*

I was ecstatic with quiet excitement. *How did you find me?*

My gaze broke to glance at the time. I had thirty minutes to get to work.

The deer didn't flinch when I stood up. She stared at me with her beautiful brown eyes.

With the time in mind, I went inside to get ready for work. I went back outside to leave and the deer was gone.

When I walked into work, I heard a loud "Welcome back, Faith!"

Immediately, everyone crowded around me for a hug. It was the last thing I'd ever expected. I managed to smile, once I got my bearings.

"Oh my, hello!"

"Oh, Faith, we're so glad you've returned. We've missed you!" Gayle giggled and gave me a hug.

Chapter 13

Three months had passed since Mom had come back into my life. My visits to see her were now a weekly ritual. I told her so much about my life.

When I wasn't working, I spent time with Gracie, talked with Terese, and explored Hill City. Though my life was full of activities, I was still lonely. I discovered an old movie theater and went there frequently. Movies had a way of massaging my heart. Their love stories rippled across the screen. Often enough, I felt like part of the movie, perhaps an extension of one of the characters that made me feel all sorts of emotions. Sometimes when a movie ended, I felt like my life paused for a while. Maybe it was a sign my life was just beginning in ways I had yet to understand. I wanted a happy ending in my own journey and my mind often drifted back to those erotic experiences with Cole.

Finding Faith

One warm and sunny mid-September day, I awoke and made my way to the bathroom where I untied my robe and let it fall to my feet. I started the water for a hot shower and glanced at myself in the full-length mirror on the door. My body seemed lighter. Still seeing its curves and dips, I appreciated it more. Slowly through the reflection, I disappeared into hot white steam.

I stepped into the shower and the warm water soothed me. It splashed up in mid-air, as droplets were suspended for a mere second before dropping down to my feet.

I had a strong desire to visit Mom again. After my shower, I dressed, ate and headed to the cemetery.

When I arrived, I remembered something I had seen earlier that week, an elderly couple holding on to each other by a pond close to St. Lucille's. This triggered a rush of emotions. I longed to be with someone again. Memories of Daniel leaving me flashed in my mind. Then fleeting images of Cole pierced through my heart. I fell down on my knees, sobbing.

"Mama!" Somehow, I managed to get into a fetal position on the ground. I held my chest, taking shallow breaths, overcome by unexpected feelings of deep sadness just beyond my consciousness. I wept some more.

"What's wrong with me, Mama?"

Just then, a breeze picked up and I heard a soft sound in the tall grass. Turning toward that sound, I noticed a piece of paper.

My sadness dissipated as I feverishly dug around the paper, folding the tall grass down and away from Mom's headstone. The paper was half buried in the dirt, so I carefully tugged it out. There were deep deposits of soil in its creases, and it was dirty, which made it look like a brown watercolor painting. There were two letters stuck together. On one letter, I read: *My Dear*...

Michael

Chapter 14

Two years earlier . . .

"Mr. Santoro, I'll see you when you get here," the woman said in a soft voice.

I grunted and quickly ended the call. When Beacon Light Nursing Home called, I knew Dad's drinking had gotten the best of him. The knots of anger buried deep inside tightened. *How dare he beckon me back, as though he still controlled me?*

Twenty minutes later, I felt queasy when I entered the nursing home. Residents were rolling down the halls in wheelchairs, monitors were buzzing, and I smelled disinfectant and body odor. A few people repeated words to themselves. I didn't even like old people. The only old person I'd ever known was Dad.

Dad began drinking heavily after Mom passed away. I was only twelve years old and he was never home. I had to learn how to cook, pack a lunch for school and clean up after myself. Dad regularly passed out on the sofa. The last time I saw him was when I was eighteen years old. Since then, he never called, and consequently, I never returned. Now, I was walking toward the room of a stranger.

I got directions to Dad's room. My throat dried up, my hands turned clammy, and my lunch balled up in the pit of my stomach. A couple seconds later, I stood at the entrance to his room and took a deep breath before facing the Old Man. The unwelcomed smells and sounds at the nursing home gave me a headache. I walked in, gagged, and stumbled into the corner of Dad's bed and grabbed my knee as I fell into the closest chair with a groan. Because of the commotion, Dad's eyelids flew open and he stared at me. I didn't know what to say, so I bent over and covered my face with my hands.

After a while, I heard someone say, "Here you go, son." A petite, older woman was standing next to me with a wet, cold rag in her hand. She was wearing a faded purple robe and white slippers. "Take this and put it on your forehead. It will help ease the pain."

Desperate for relief, I grabbed the cloth and put it on my head. The cool wetness stopped my head from spinning.

"Thank you," I groaned. The woman walked out of the room.

I looked up to see Dad staring back at me with deep, brown, distant eyes. It was difficult to tell if the man lying in the bed was indeed my father. He had dropped twenty pounds. Thick, blue veins protruded from his arms. His face was skeletal.

"Hello, Dad," I managed to say.

He mumbled something. When I didn't answer, he asked in a loud whisper, "Who *are* you?"

Dumbfounded, I looked at him and my blood began

to boil. It was one thing not to be acknowledged as a child after Mom's passing, but here we were, years later and he didn't have a clue who I was.

"I'm Michael. Your *son*," I said between clenched teeth.

His eyes glanced around the room. Again, as if not hearing me, he asked, "Who *are* you?"

I sat motionless, his three-word question slapping me in the face. I wasn't going to allow this man to put me down anymore. I rose to my feet and walked out of the room.

I was so angry; my skin was on fire. For years, I had kept this pain locked up, ignored, and buried deep down inside.

As I ran down the hall, that pain surfaced. Looking at the ground, I suppressed the tears that were about to explode. *I have to get out of here! I have to get out!* I was determined not to show any sort of emotion for this man.

In my frantic attempt to escape, I bumped into someone so hard, I knocked her to the floor. Everyone looked at me.

"Oh my gosh! Are you okay? I'm so sorry. Are you okay?" I faked a concern.

"Oh my," she said in a high-pitched voice.

A rush of nurses came over and pushed me aside. In my selfish attempt to escape, I had knocked over an elderly woman.

I recognized her voice from earlier. She was the one in Dad's room with me.

"Let me help you back to your room. Are you okay with that, ma'am? That's the least I could do."

"Sir, we can't let you do that," one of the nurses said. "We'll take her back to her room."

Another nurse hurried over with a wheelchair and carefully helped her get into it.

"You can walk with us." The old woman winked. I followed as she was wheeled to the opposite end of the hall.

The last thing I need is a lawsuit! The door at the end of the hall was hers. I glanced at the nameplate. It was blank.

The woman pointed to the circular brown chair next to the window. "You can sit over there."

I dragged the seat closer to her wheelchair. "Miss, would you mind leaving us alone for a few minutes?" I asked.

The nurse nodded and left the room.

The woman was wearing the same faded purple robe and white slippers. I was drawn to her baby blue eyes and petite stature.

"I'm very sorry, ma'am."

"What's with the ma'am business? You can call me Lina. And who might you be?"

"I'm Michael. It's nice to meet you, Lina. I'm sorry we had to be introduced this way," I said, trying to sound apologetic.

Lina smiled and said, "I love the name Michael. It's one of my favorite names."

Chapter 15

After Dad hadn't recognized me, two years ago, I fled the Beacon Light Nursing Home, never expecting to return. *I was such a coward!*

Now, as I look out the window at my hotel, memories of my life with him have resurfaced.

"Mr. Santoro, your room is ready," the hotel manager said as he gave me my room key.

"Thank you. I will mosey up there shortly."

I was transfixed on a family outside, unpacking their bright blue Outback Subaru. When I heard the excitement in the children's voices and saw how happy the husband and wife were, I thought about what was missing from my childhood.

Before Mom got sick, the three of us spent a lot of time together as a family. I relished having been loved as a child, fondly recalling Mom during those years. She stayed home and took care of me while Dad worked at a car dealership.

The worst day of my life was when Mom died of cancer.

Anger seethed inside of me as I recalled how quickly Dad's personality changed.

Bitter memories from my last visit to the nursing home were still fresh in my mind. I grabbed my bags, took the elevator to my hotel room, and reluctantly unlocked the door.

As I walked in, the phone rang. It was a call from Beacon Light Nursing Home. They said Dad was in pretty bad shape and it sounded like he didn't have much time.

On my way to the nursing home, I felt like I was going to throw up. I flexed my hands, alternating left and right. I've always wondered what kind of people surrendered themselves to such a dreary place and now I know one.

When I was eighteen years old, I got my big break to get out of this town. Even though he was my father, he never really cared for me after Mom died.

Once I arrived, I went to the nurse's station to get this over with. The nurse in charge recognized me.

"Hello, Mr. Santoro." She gave a stern smirk. "We've been trying to contact you since the last time you came, but haven't been able to reach you until now." She looked down and shuffled papers, giving me the cold shoulder.

"Oh," I paused, remembering those calls I chose to ignore. I lied and said, "I'm sorry. My job takes me all over the place and I'm hard to track down."

Without looking up, she said, "Well, your father has been in and out of a coma since you left last time. We rarely see people hang on this long, but he has."

I choked on my saliva. "What—in and out of a coma?"

"That's what I said, Mr. Santoro," she snapped. "Since your father listed you in his Health Care Directive, you'll need to make the decision to—"

"Make what decision?"

"Well," she took a long deep breath, and said, "you need to decide if he should stay or pass on if he doesn't come out of his coma or his body weakens."

Why would Dad have me in his Health Care Directive when he doesn't remember me? My hunch was right. He was on his last leg. I tried to digest what she had said and began to get upset. *This was his ultimate power over me, and, damn, I wasn't going to make that decision! He can rot in hell!*

"Could you just tell me where he is?"

She said the room number and pointed down the hall.

Dad appeared even smaller and thinner than I had remembered. Now the only difference was that a machine helped him breathe and an assortment of tubes were connected to him. Beeping noises sounded in the background. He looked pale and lifeless. I sat down in a chair by the window and put my head in my hands.

"You've come back," a woman's voice quietly said, catching me off guard.

"Huh?" I looked up and saw the same woman from the last time I visited Dad.

Embarrassed, I straightened in my chair and held my head high.

"Oh. Yes, I'm back."

"We wondered what happened to you. Is it Michael? I remember your name because I like it." She smiled.

"Yes, it is. And you are . . ." *What was her name?*

"Lina," she said with a smile.

"Ah yes, Lina."

"Hal, look who came to see you. Michael's back," she said, looking at Dad.

I hadn't heard his name in such a long time.

"Hal can hear us talk; he just can't respond. The coma, you know." Lina glanced at me.

"How has he been?" I surprised myself with that question, but figured I needed to avoid talking about what happened last time.

"Your father, he is a strong man. He's become weaker since he's been here though."

"Yes, so I've heard," I mumbled.

She perked up and said, "Oh my, I just remembered something. I'll be right back!" She waddled out of the room.

That was awkward. I shifted my focus to Dad again. There was nothing about him that looked familiar. The man looked like he was dying. His face was expressionless; his eyes were closed and he was breathing through a machine.

When I was a kid, he drank a lot and was depressed. I guess he quit his job and drank himself here. I was angry at him all over again for abandoning me when I was young and for not remembering me last time. *Why am I here again? I should've just stayed in Las Vegas.*

I've begun to dislike my job over these past few years. As a tourism representative for a popular hotel and casino, I didn't sleep much and I experienced vices I wouldn't have known had I not accepted that position. Sexy women, flashy nightclubs, and entertainment galore were at my disposal. I was treated like a king with free food, travel and hotel stays. In the beginning, it provided me with freedom, and for the first time since Mom's passing, I felt like I belonged again.

But over the last few years, everything about this job that once attracted me started to wear on me. I was always traveling, never staying in one place, and I didn't like who I had become.

"Oh, dear, I almost forgot about this," Lina chimed as she walked back into the room, startling me.

What's she talking about?

"Michael, when your dad was awake, we talked about you."

"Really?" I was baffled. *Who is this woman and why does she have so much information about Dad?*

"He was upset for not remembering you the last time you were here," she said, trying to convince me. "Surprisingly, he goes in and out of consciousness at times, something the nurses hadn't seen before, which tells me he's hanging on."

"He remembered me? His son?"

She laughed quietly and said, "Yes, he did. He remembered you."

Upon hearing this news, the anger I had for years started to melt away. I looked over at Dad, and, for the first time in a very long while, I felt a little compassion for the man.

"But that's not all," Lina said, looking at me waiting for my reaction.

"What do you mean?"

"Your father gave me something to give to you. He wasn't sure you'd ever come back, but if you did, he asked me to pass it on." Lina took her hands from behind her back and handed me a small manila envelope.

Chapter 16

I slowly turned the envelope over, reached inside, and pulled out a silver key. I was intrigued. I looked at Lina, who shrugged apologetically.

"What's this?"

"It looks like a key to me," she said with a smile.

"I know it's a key, but for what?"

"Well, when you find out, we should talk. How long are you staying?" Lina paused at the door.

"Oh, I'm not sure. It really depends on Dad's condition."

I wondered what the key meant, and fingered it before sliding it into my pocket.

We said goodbye and I turned my attention back to the key. I had an idea and left the nursing home.

I had almost forgotten the directions to the house where I lived when I was a child, but as I drove around, I found my way back. Though I didn't want to go anywhere near that place, it was suddenly important to find out why Dad left me a key.

Our split-level home looked unkempt. The old white paint was peeling on the outside and vines were crawling up the gutters. Mom would've had a fit. Several days of newspapers had accumulated on the front steps and the mail bulged out of the door slot. *Who has been looking after his house?*

With the curtains drawn, it looked unoccupied and forlorn, the perfect place for a burglary. I couldn't believe Dad would let this happen to our home. Then again, alcohol and depression had become his new roommates.

I walked around the house, hoping to find an unlocked back door or an open window. Smells of decaying garbage lingered in the air. I quickly walked back to the front again.

I saw a crinkled CONDEMNED sign on the door. I took a photo of it with my cell phone hoping to call the number later.

I pulled the silver key out of my pocket, hoping it was the key to our house. I put the key into the rusty, old knob on the front door. I jiggled the doorknob as I gently moved the key around in the chamber. After several attempts, the door sprang open.

I slowly entered the dark and dreary house. *Why did Dad give me a key to our home?* Suddenly, I tripped over a flashlight and caught myself. I picked it up and pushed the on button. Old newspapers were piled high on the coffee table. Spoiled food stunk up the house. *This is disgusting!*

I had to breathe through my mouth to avoid gagging. I wandered through what used to be our home, trying to hold my breath so as not to smell the stench. I pulled the curtains to the side and tried to open the windows, but they were painted shut. A sticky mess clung to the front face of the fan. I turned it on and miraculously, it worked. There were scattered magazines, golf balls, blankets, and clothes on the floors. The bathroom and bedrooms were cluttered with junk. Dad's bed sheets had obviously not been changed in years and there were yellow-stained blankets lying on the floor. Water stains spotted the ceilings. In the hall closet, I found a can of lemon-scented Lysol disinfectant, so I sprayed it in the bedroom and the bathroom. There were a few large black plastic garbage bags in the kitchen cupboard. The place smelled like vomit. Empty bottles of cheap vodka, brandy, beer, and wine were lying around.

My attempt to clean the place was exhausting, mentally and physically. After two hours, I took out the trash, grabbed the Lysol and sprayed it all over the house. Within minutes, the main floor smelled of lemons.

I put it off all afternoon, but I couldn't avoid it any longer; I had to go to my old room. *What had Dad done with it after all these years?*

My bedroom was downstairs, along with my own bathroom and living area. After Mom passed, I don't remember Dad ever coming down there. I didn't know what to expect.

On the way down to my room, I waded through more garbage that lined the stairs—beer bottles, stained and torn books stripped of their bindings, stale fish food with visible white mold and a few couch pillows. I finally made it down the stairs. The living area was also a pigsty, so I expected even worse in my bedroom. *Oh, what the hell!*

I pushed the door to my bedroom and it creaked open. The carpeted floor was clean and vacuumed. I opened the door a bit more and stepped inside. It was an amazing sight. Memories of my youth flooded back. My room looked exactly the same as it did the day I said goodbye and left for the big city. Tears blurred my vision. My twin bed with the blue comforter was neatly made just as it was when I left home. The few trinkets on my dresser were dusty, yet untouched. My closet held a few old clothes, but they were ironed just as I'd left them.

I felt a twinge of guilt knowing that two years ago I had stormed out of Dad's room at the nursing home like a two-year old during a temper tantrum. *Shit, I need to stop running!*

Surveying the room, preserved like a time capsule, my eye caught something that seemed out of place. Extending beyond the tan carpet that covered most of the floor, ending right beneath the window, was something red, almost like a wide ribbon. I had no idea what it was.

I knelt down and tugged at the piece of cloth until it tore off. I peeled back the carpet and had to lift the bed to see it better. Once the carpet was pulled back, I stared down in disbelief. There, I saw a small box with a handle carved into the floor.

Chapter 17

While I was visiting Dad the next day, Lina came into his room and sat down next to me.

"Hi," I said, still wondering about the box in the bedroom floor.

Lina smiled and took Dad's hand in hers. She lifted her head and tenderly looked into my eyes. Dad was fading fast.

"Lina, would you be able to take a short walk with me?" I hoped to lift the veil around her. "I could use a break."

"Sure, son," she said, putting Dad's hand back under the blanket.

We walked outside, where it was oddly quiet, so unlike the noise I was accustomed to in Las Vegas.

"So, Lina, how do you know Dad?"

"Well . . ." She squinted up at me through the sunlight. "Hal and I go way back. We met at a barn dance years ago. When he checked into Beacon Light, we reconnected."

"Oh, I see. Do you know when Dad's health began to deteriorate?"

"The doctors said he began to go downhill since your last visit."

Immediately, I felt defeated. "I'm sorry, but I don't get how any of this is my fault!" I tried to remain calm, but it was difficult. "First, my own dad doesn't recognize me. Then he was in and out of a coma, and has deteriorated after I left this place two years ago? I'm so sick and tired of being blamed for his crap!"

Calmly, Lina interjected, "I know all of this is very difficult for you, Michael. I sense there's still a lot of pain and confusion about what happened to you and your family. May I offer a different perspective? When Hal was well, we often talked about his life. Surprisingly, once he quit drinking and became more stable with medication and treatment, he opened up to me."

"Oh?"

"Your dad loved your mom very much. When she died, a part of him went with her. She was the love of his life. Your dad said that when they had you, they were happy, but when your mom was ill, he was beside himself, unsure how to help her. He could no longer keep your mom safe. As she was dying, his world shrunk. Even though I've spent time getting reacquainted with your dad, he always had a distant longing look in his eyes, as though he was not fully present, as though a part of him was with your mom."

I nodded, wanting to hear more.

"When your mom died, he didn't know what to do anymore. He undoubtedly loved you and that never changed, but he felt useless and immobilized by his failure to save your mother. I remember when we talked about this, he broke down in front of me. He was remorseful. Not only had he lost your mom, his only child was gone too."

Now, tears spilled down my face as memories of this heartbreak swept over me. I wiped at my eyes with my shirt sleeve and, clearing my throat, I choked, "Please, continue."

"Hal never thought he would see you again. He felt like a failure as a husband and a father. When you decided to move away, he couldn't blame you. He didn't want you to go, yet, he didn't know how to ask you to stay. When you came back, I thought his prayers were answered. Then, when you left again, he lost hope. He was sure you'd never come back. He was ashamed for not recognizing you that day."

I never imagined I'd hear words of apology from anyone, especially Dad.

"This is a lot to absorb, isn't it?"

I nodded and choked on my tears.

Lina looped her arm through mine, and we continued our walk.

"I wish your father could tell you all of this, and I'm sure he won't mind that I'm his messenger. Michael, please try to accept what I'm telling you. Nothing was ever your fault. Your mom was very ill. Her death still stirs up a lot of pain for your father. He never stopped loving you. Deep down he wants to see you again. I continue to pray that he wakes up." She wiped a few tears from her eyes.

"Thank you for telling me this. I'm glad he had a friend to talk to. I had no idea." I was overwhelmed and I needed time to digest this unexpected information.

"Let's go back to your dad's room. I'll leave you two alone."

I nodded, my mouth dry.

When we got to Dad's door, I remembered the box. "Lina before you go, can you tell me anything about that key that Dad gave me? I don't understand what it's for. I went to our house and it opened the front door. I also found a box in my bedroom floor, but I don't know what it is."

"I don't know anything about that key, but I do know the front door has been open for years," Lina said, as she turned and walked away.

Chapter 18

I was puzzled by what Lina had revealed and turned my attention to Dad. He lay in bed frail and motionless, eyes closed. A breathing machine continued to pump oxygen into his lungs, while IVs, feeding tubes and monitors kept his body functioning. My heart was heavy that Dad's tenuous hold on life seemed to depend on these impersonal machines.

I sat near his bed and looked at him for the longest time. His face looked pale, and his mouth hung slack. He looked suspended between life and death.

For the first time in years, I was alone with him. A cool breeze graced my neck. *Are you here, Mom?*

"Hi, Dad. I'm here." The words easily flew out of my mouth. "I just went on a long walk with Lina. She's a remarkable woman. She said things you've never told me. I'm so sorry for not being a better son and for leaving when I should've stayed. I know there's been a lot of wasted time between us and I regret that." When I looked at him, nothing had changed. A slight breeze swept across the back of my head again.

"Mom, I hope you're here, watching over Dad and me. I love you," I whispered, rubbing the back of my head.

∞ ∞

Back at my childhood home a couple hours later, I was magnetically drawn to the box in the bedroom floor, but I was emotionally exhausted. I went to sleep, planning to deal with the mystery box in the morning.

My phone startled me out of a deep sleep. "Hello?"

"Mr. Santoro? This is Lynda at the nursing home. We need you to come quickly."

Flustered, I got dressed and hurried to see Dad. I didn't know what had happened, but I prepared myself for the worst.

Lynda was waiting for me. "Good morning Mr. Santoro, I'm glad you're here. Your dad's nurse needs to speak with you right away."

I raced down the hall and a nurse intercepted me on the way. "We've seen small movements in your dad's hands and legs, twitching if you will. This rarely happens and is the reason for our early morning call."

Elated by this news, I walked briskly into Dad's room. No one was there, so I closed the door and took a seat by his bedside.

"Hi, Dad, it's me, Michael. I'm here now." I felt odd talking to someone who couldn't answer me.

I looked at him for a long while and a slight breeze tickled the back of my neck. It had to be Mom. I felt comforted.

I watched Dad's hands and legs hoping for any sort of movement and then glanced at his eyes, which were still closed.

I jumped up at a knock at the door. Lina walked into the room.

"Hey, Lina."

"Good morning, Michael. I heard the news about Hal. I'm so excited. How is he?"

"I just got here and there's no movement yet. Since last night, I've felt a cool breeze on my neck. What do you suppose that is?"

"Without a question, your mom. Your dad felt that too."

"Really?" For the first time in a long while, I smiled.

I continued to chat with Lina. She explained that yesterday wore her out and we laughed when we discovered we had both crashed.

"So, what's your story, Lina? Are you married? Do you have kids? What filled your life before coming here?" I had many questions for her, now more than ever.

We decided to continue our talk somewhere else, so we left Dad for a while, and headed to the cafeteria for a snack and something to drink. The nurse said she would page me if we needed to return to his room.

"Well, I've never been married but I had a child out of wedlock, which, back then, was sinful. While I loved the man, he didn't stick around and left by the time our Bree was three."

"Wow, that must've been hard for you."

With our coffees and muffins in hand, we walked back to Dad's room. I hadn't been paged so I was hoping no news was good news.

"And Bree, where is she now?"

Just as we turned the corner, Dad's nurse came rushing towards us. "Come quick you two! Your dad is awake!"

Wide-eyed, we looked at each other and then ran to Dad's room. Sure enough, his eyes were open.

Lina and I sat on either side of Dad's bed and we each held one of his hands. "Dad, can you see me?"

I wasn't prepared for this turn of events. I glanced at Lina silently begging for help because he wasn't responding.

"Sweet Hal—are you awake? Can you hear me?" Lina echoed.

At that moment, Dad turned his head to look at Lina. I sat unmoving, hoping he heard her. Dad's mouth opened but nothing came out. Lina reached for a glass of water and trickled a small sip into his mouth. Dad coughed.

"He squeezed my hand—" Lina gasped in delight.

"Dad," I interrupted. "I'm here too."

Sadly, Dad's gaze didn't leave Lina's face nor did he squeeze my hand. I let go of his hand and walked over next to Lina. He didn't blink but stared off into a place far behind us.

I looked down to hide the guilt and shame that still filled me. Just then, a voice startled me.

"Be - th."

Dad spoke! He said Mom's name! Holy crap! I hadn't heard anyone say her name in such a long time. I felt the cool breeze and knew Mom was here with us.

"Hal, Beth is here too. And your son, Michael."

Dad blinked and focused his deep brown eyes on me. I froze. His gaze pierced through me. I inhaled sharply.

After what seemed like five long minutes, Dad spoke in a raspy voice. "I love you, Michael."

I almost fell over hearing the words I had longed for

since childhood. I wanted him to say it again and again so I could remember this moment forever.

His gaze turned from me to Lina. To her, he whispered, "Thank you," and then he closed his eyes.

I rose to my feet and ran as fast as I could out of that room, which suddenly felt too crowded and claustrophobic.

My head was about to burst. Despite my efforts to mask my feelings and bury them deep inside, I knew I couldn't do that any longer. Once outside, I kept running, past my car, to a wide and open sandy field beyond the nursing home. I collapsed onto the ground and started to wail. I grabbed my chest and rocked in the dirt. The hurt I'd been feeling all these years penetrated through my body.

A cool breeze tickled the back of my neck. *Please help me, Mom. I know you're here.*

Chapter 19

I mustered up the energy to stand and drive to the house. Once I got there, I went inside and removed my shoes. I put my cell phone in my right shoe, went to my bedroom, collapsed into bed, and fell asleep.

Early the next morning, my cell phone rang. I ran to grab it from my shoe. As soon as I picked it up, it stopped ringing. The call was from Beacon Light Nursing Home. My heart hammered in my chest as I listened to the voicemail. It was a nurse who spoke urgently, saying Dad's heart might be failing and to come quickly.

Once I got to Beacon Light, I raced down the hall and into Dad's room. His eyes were closed, and his chest was barely moving. The beep beep beep on the heart monitor caught my attention. Dad's heart was beating at a much slower pace.

I pulled the chair over to his bed and sat next to him. I

was flooded with emotions as I remembered my outburst from yesterday.

Just then, Lina walked in. "Hello, Michael," she said quietly, shuffling over to sit next to me. "He doesn't look well, does he?"

I nodded and looked over at Dad. His face was yellowish and his lips had turned light blue. I touched his hand. "His hand is really cold."

"I'm going to find one of the nurses," Lina said as she walked out of the room.

Could this be it? Is he dying? I didn't know what to do with myself. The only time I had ever been with someone who was dying was when I was with Mom. My hands started to sweat and my breath was shallow.

One of the nurses came in to check Dad's vitals. She looked at me and said, "Your dad doesn't have much time, but he probably has a few hours."

Lina looked at the nurse. Then she looked at me. The nurse left the room.

I took a deep breath and moaned, "Oh no, I can't believe it. Did I hear her right?"

Lina nodded, "Yes, you did."

Yesterday, Dad woke up from his coma and now he only has a few hours left? Even though I hated the person he became after Mom died, I wasn't ready to say goodbye.

As Lina watched the waves of confusion on my face, she said, "Let's go get a cup of coffee. We'll be down the hall, so if anything happens, they'll come and get us."

I stood up, nodding in agreement. I always began my day with strong coffee and knew I would need a clear head to get through today.

When we were out of his room and within the smell of coffee, I snapped out of my fog. "I'm sorry, Lina. I just didn't expect Dad to die so suddenly. I'm not as prepared as I thought I'd be."

"Son, it's alright. No one can predict when someone dies, so we'll just see what happens," Lina said reassuringly. She paid for our coffee.

"So, yesterday you were going to tell me about your daughter Bree. How old is she? Does she live close?" I asked, trying to find a distraction.

"Ah, my Bree." She smiled, reached into her pocket and pulled out a photo to show me. She had long, dark-blonde hair, blue eyes, and a wonderful smile.

"Wow, she's beautiful."

"Yes she is. She's my only child. She looks a lot like me."

"I see that. Tell me more about her."

"Well, it's sad. I don't know much about her anymore. She stopped talking to me. But I always pray she'll return to find me."

"Oh my. What happened, if I may ask?"

"I'm not sure." Lina looked away and wiped a tear from her eye.

"This must be difficult to talk about. I'm sorry I brought it up."

"I still love her, and if I were well enough and had the money, I would track her down. My memory isn't as sharp as it used to be, but I'll always love her. She's the love of my life."

∞ ∞

I spent the next week checking in on Dad and learning more about Bree. As I heard about how much Lina loved

Bree, I was starting to develop feelings for Bree even though we hadn't met.

Dad was back in a coma and death seemed hours away. But hours turned into days and days turned into weeks. His breathing and heart rate became erratic. His vital signs slowly diminished and then quickly rebounded in a never-ending cycle.

I was scheduled to fly back to Las Vegas. I didn't know what that meant for my relationship with Dad. Since he was awake briefly, uttered Mom's name, and told me he loved me, I was hoping he would come out of the coma again.

I wanted to see Dad one last time before I had to leave for my flight, so I got dressed, ate breakfast, and drove to Beacon Light Nursing Home.

When I got there, I walked into Dad's room. All I could hear was the breathing machine. Conscious of the time, I sat near his bed and took his hand in mine.

"Dad, I have to go back to Las Vegas."

Nothing happened, not even a flinch. I tried not to think this was a waste of time but that's what I believed. Most of my trip had been spent getting to know Lina and cleaning up Dad's house.

As if on cue, Lina poked her graying head in the doorway. "How is he?"

"The same," I said, my voice plummeting.

"I'm so sorry, Michael. I thought he would be awake by now." Lina walked over to me and gave me a big hug.

"Me too. Thank you for being here for me and for all you shared with me about my parents and your daughter."

We said our goodbyes and I asked Lina to call me if there were any changes.

I was only a few miles from the airport when my phone rang.

"Hello?"

"Michael, turn around and come back! Your Dad is awake and he's asking for you," Lina said, frantically.

I smiled. Dad's timing was always off. I made a U-turn in the middle of the road and sped back to the nursing home. My mind was racing. I had to catch my flight in three hours and I didn't want to miss it. At the same time, Dad was asking for me. I needed to go back.

I parked and ran as fast as I could to Dad's room. I almost lost it. His room was empty. I was too late.

"Michael, you made it!" Lina poked her head out of another room. She looked confused by my expression of disappointment. She ran over, grabbed my arm, and led me into the room where she had been.

He's alive!

I walked over to Dad's bedside and Lina said, "I'm going to let you two have some privacy. You'll be okay. Just talk with him."

I looked at Dad, who appeared to be on the last leg of his journey. I didn't know if he was awake, asleep, or if he could hear me.

I felt a cool breeze on the back of my neck. Mom was with us. Almost instantly, I felt calm. My jitters were gone and my pulse had slowed down.

"Dad, I'm here. I've come to see you again. I'm so sorry for leaving when I was younger, for not contacting you, and for giving up on you. I remember how we were when Mom was alive. I loved our family back then and can't think of a time since when I've been happier." I started to cry, realizing this was likely the last time I'd be able to talk with him.

I pushed myself to continue. "When Mom died, it was devastating for us. I didn't know what to do. I was just a kid. No matter how sad I was to see Mom go, I needed you more than ever. My worst fears proved to be true because when Mom died, a part of you went with her. Every year after that, I developed more dislike for you and for myself. I lived through my grief alone. It was as if your ghost lived at the house. When I looked at you, I saw someone I didn't recognize. I didn't know what to do. So, when I turned eighteen, I left and never wanted to look back. Now that I'm here, everything is clearer and I need to be here with you. Wait. Not need. Want. Yes, I want to be here with you." I wiped the tears from my face, afraid someone would barge into his room.

I took a sip of water.

"If we could go back, I'd do things differently. I love you and Mom very much. I'm so sorry I abandoned you. I wish I'd have been more patient and let time heal us. But I was full of self-righteousness and I blamed you for everything wrong in my life. I can't believe you're almost gone and there's nothing I can do to change that." My chest heaved as I tried to catch my breath.

To my surprise, I heard the sound of a raspy old voice. Dad was using his last bit of strength to speak to me. His eyes were opening and I saw the Dad I had grown up with before Mom died. Tears streamed down my face as he lifted his hand just enough for me to grasp it. He squeezed my hand as hard as he could, even though his grip was weak.

Dad fumbled for words but his eyes never left mine. "Michael, I will . . . will . . . always love . . . love you. I'm so sorry for . . . for . . . hurting you. You've always been the light . . . light of my life."

After a few harsh coughs he continued, almost in a whisper, "I want to . . . to go to . . . to your mother now. We will always be . . . be with you, son."

Dad's eyes closed, his hand let go of mine and he stopped breathing. Everything happened so fast, but I was finally at peace. I sat next to him for at least another twenty minutes, quietly crying for all the times we could've spent together.

The last few minutes of his life had become the most important minutes of mine.

Chapter 20

I canceled my flight home. Lina and I wanted to do something in memory of Dad. He had made it clear to Lina that he didn't want a service of any kind, and I couldn't imagine who would even come. Lina had a place she wanted to go for a picnic to honor him.

As I drove to pick up Lina, I had mixed feelings. My eyes filled with tears when I least expected, and I was overcome with emotion, missing the dad I had known long ago and regretting not having the chance to get to know him better.

Dad's last wish was to be with Mom, which comforted me. I was glad I could apologize to him and tell him I never stopped loving him.

"I can't wait to show you this place," Lina said with obvious anticipation while I helped her into the car.

"Well, you'll have to tell me where we're going so I can get us there." Now that Dad had died, I felt a weight lift off my shoulders. The sun was shining and it was warm enough for shorts.

"So, how are you feeling, Michael? Are you okay with this?"

"I don't know. I feel a little bit of everything, but I'm glad that I made peace with Dad before he died. When I first arrived, my body ached and I was so upset. Now, I feel more settled and centered. It helped to hear that Dad wanted to be with Mom, and that he loved me. I'm glad I was able to come back home and face my demons."

Lina directed us to a beautiful place on a hill overlooking rugged valleys of rock formations dotted with tall green pine trees. It was a lookout I never knew existed. I brought a basket with sandwiches, oranges and juice. We sat at a picnic table and I took out our lunch. There was a warm breeze and birds chirped in nearby trees. During lunch, we talked about Dad's friendship with Lina. They were good friends, but as Lina reminded me, he was sick for a long time.

"Hal missed your mom every day. Picturing them together now gives me joy in spite of the pain," Lina said.

"I guess I was spared the sense of devastation with Dad's death because we had little communication and I hadn't bothered to form a relationship of any kind except an icy standoff. Still, I'm sad that we lost so much time together."

"I know what you mean," Lina said.

The conversation turned again to Lina's daughter, Bree. I was glad Lina could open up about Bree. Amazingly, she had no hard feelings about her daughter, even though Bree hadn't bothered to call or show up. Lina expressed a lot of grace when she talked about Bree. She held onto those fond memories instead of dwelling on the sad ones.

While Lina talked about her daughter, I was slowly getting to know Bree and I reflected on what was missing in my own life. I wanted something more for myself and I longed to meet someone with whom I could build a life and find that kind of deep love my parents had for each other. But I was always traveling, not able to lay down roots. Now, I entertained the idea of settling down and having a family.

"I can tell how much you love Bree. I wish she'd kept in touch with you. It bothers me that she hasn't come back into your life," I said to Lina. I had almost been too late for Dad and I feared Bree might be too late if she didn't come around soon. Watching Lina talk, I noticed how tired she looked. Maybe it was my preoccupation with Dad's passing, but today, Lina looked much older.

Before she could respond, I said, "I think we should get going. I had a wonderful time. Thank you for bringing me here and for all your support before Dad passed."

"I was glad to be there for him, and for you. I miss coming to this beautiful spot where I can see the sun rise and set. It has always given me a chance to see the day begin and end. I had a good time with you today."

On our way home, I was thinking about all I had learned about Lina and Bree, and my own feelings about Dad. I couldn't wait for my life to move forward.

"You never told me about the key your dad gave you. Whatever happened to it?" Lina asked.

"Oh, gosh. I forgot about the key in all the commotion with Dad. I forgot about the box, too."

"What box?" Lina's fatigue was suddenly replaced with excitement.

"Let me start from the beginning. The key helped to

open the door to our house, but then you said the door had always been open, so I don't know what happened, but the door didn't open without it. The last thing I remember is this red cloth attached to a box under my bedroom floor. When I pulled the cloth, it tore off. Now, I'm eager to find out about that box."

"Take me with you, please? I want to see it too," she begged.

I couldn't resist her excitement. I drove to Dad's house so we could solve this mystery together.

When we got to the house, we went inside. "Be careful," I warned. "There's a lot of stuff still in here, so hang onto me as we walk through, okay?"

We walked down the stairs and into my old bedroom. "Oh my, you did such a good job cleaning this place. I came here many times to check on it and it was a mess."

"Yes, it was. Can you tell me anything about the condemned notice on the front door? What's that about? I forgot to call the number on the sign."

"Oh, yes, your dad's house will be condemned soon. I forgot to tell you that. He kept asking me to appeal the order because of you, so I tried to get to the house whenever I could. He wanted you to come here. I now know why."

I turned to look at her. She winked at me. *The key, of course.*

"I'm so glad you're here with me. I don't know what I'd do without your care and insight," I said, as I led her into my bedroom and pointed to the box carved into the floor.

Lina gasped, "Oh boy! This is exciting!"

We knelt on the floor and pulled the handle on the outside of the box. With our combined strength, it popped

Finding Faith

open. Inside was another wooden box with a lock. We looked at each other, wide eyed.

"Well, aren't you going to open it?" Lina whispered, interrupting my thoughts.

Curiosity grabbed me. Reaching into my pocket, I pulled out the key and inserted it. The key turned smoothly and the box sprung open. To my surprise, there was a dark blue box inside. I lifted it out of the wooden case. It was sealed with duct tape.

"What the heck?"

"Look!" Lina said. "There's something else in there!"

I looked down and found a note. I opened it and read it aloud.

Michael, please take this box with you and open it when you are back home and alone. Your mom and I love you very much and we are always with you.

I broke down and cried.

Lina put her arm around me and tried to cradle me to the best of her petite ability. She was crying, too. I had no idea what was in the box, but it was surreal seeing Dad's handwriting scribbled on that piece of paper. I soaked in his words of love.

I drove Lina back to the nursing home, where we hugged and said our second goodbyes.

This time, I was able to catch my return flight to Las Vegas. On the plane, I was quiet and reflective while the box sat securely in my lap.

After I returned to Las Vegas, I reflected on my visit to see Dad. I had been transformed on every level of my being, thanks to Lina. My inner restlessness was finally calm and

I had begun a journey to rebuild my life and rediscover myself. I now saw with new eyes how I was meant to live and I knew, somehow, I would become whole at last.

I had to jump back into the entertainment world of work and didn't have time to check on Lina or open the box from my bedroom. Sadly, two weeks after I returned to Las Vegas, Beacon Light called to say Lina had passed away quietly in her sleep. On hearing the news, I cried for Bree, who likely hadn't had the chance to visit her mom before she died.

I started to pray again, something I hadn't done since the day Mom died. Through prayer, I felt relief from sadness and lost time, even for Lina, a beautiful woman whom I knew only in bits and pieces, but with whom I felt surprisingly close. I sent Beacon Light Nursing Home flowers in her honor.

A month later, a package arrived. Inside were Dad's and Lina's ashes and another envelope. In Dad's handwriting it was labeled, *To My Beloved Son, Michael.*

His words tugged on my heartstrings. Inside the envelope was a check for two hundred thousand dollars.

Faith

Chapter 21

*T*erese left me a voicemail. "Hi, Faith, Do you realize it's been a year since you moved to Arizona? I think we need to celebrate, so I bought you a ticket to the Big Apple. Let's spend the weekend together."

༄ ༄

When I walked out of the airport, I spotted Terese's Jeep. Immediately, the chilly air nipped at my nose. I had forgotten how much colder it is in New York City.

"Hi, Faith! I'm so glad to see you!" Terese hugged me and put my luggage in the trunk.

"Hi! Nice to see you too. Holy Hannah, it's cold out here!" I said, zipping up my jacket.

"I'm sure winters are warmer in Hill City. Come, get in the car. Let's get out of here." We got into her Jeep.

"So, how've you been? I feel like we haven't caught up in ages," Terese said.

"Oh, good. Everything is about the same, except I found something." I looked over at Terese, waiting for her reaction.

"Oh, really? What's that?"

"I've been visiting Mom at the cemetery and I found two letters by her gravestone. I think they're from someone who liked her. But, it's weird because she died a year ago, so, who would be putting love letters there?"

"Wait a minute. Love letters? Did you read them?" I had Terese's full attention.

"I've read one."

"Oh my goodness! What did it say and what happened to the other one?"

"I thought the first letter only said My Dear . . . but then, after I scraped the dirt off, I could read more of it."

I pulled it out of my pocket and continued to read it to Terese.

I wish we had met sooner. I would've wrapped you up and kept you close. My senses have come alive like never before. I wish I could see you again. Love . . .

"Hey!" Terese slapped my arm softly. "How cool is that?" Terese was obviously more excited than I was. "So, what about the other letter? What did it say?"

I cringed. "I didn't read it."

"Why? I don't understand." Terese's tone plummeted.

"I just found out about my mom, the accident with Daniel, and my memory loss. I don't want to know about the lover Mom left behind. My mom is dead. If some jerk wrote her letters, I sure as hell don't care!" I stammered, feeling my blood boil. "I just haven't been in the mood to read the stupid letters."

Terese revved up the engine. Without a word, she drove back to her penthouse.

Once we were in the underground parking garage, I said softly, "Terese, I'm sorry for having a fit back there. Let's not talk about the letters, right now, okay? I just want to relax."

As if forcing out her words, Terese said, "It's okay. I shouldn't have pushed it with you. I've been stressed lately, too, and I was hoping to hear some excitement in your life. But that's okay. I won't bring it up again."

When we got to her apartment, I suggested, "Can we go to that same bar we went to the last time I was here? You know, the one where we had anonymous flings with strangers? I need a drink."

"Good idea," she said.

This time, we didn't change into elegant clothes. Instead, we took turns touching up our makeup and brushing our hair before we left. The only thing on my mind was a cold beer. I wanted to wash down the bad taste in my mouth from our earlier conversation.

When we got to Gaby's Nightclub, the place was packed. By chance, the same table we sat at last time was open, so we sat down. It was happy hour, so drinks were two for one. I ordered beer and Terese ordered wine. We clanked our glasses together and took a sip. We didn't need to talk, so we sat in silence as we drank our drinks. I finished mine in fifteen minutes. Terese trailed behind me, finishing hers in twenty. When I stood up, I felt queasy.

"I'm going to the bathroom," I yelled. Inside the ladies' room, I held onto the stall door because the room was beginning to spin. *Why is this happening? I only had two drinks, and they were beers!* I hadn't eaten much. I camped out in the bathroom for ten minutes until I felt well enough to return to the table.

As I made my way back to the table, I noticed Terese wasn't there. I was still annoyed with her for pressing me about the letters. I sat down and ate some popcorn. Within a few minutes, I felt better. I ordered another beer. Terese bumped into the back of my chair.

"Hey," she slurred. "I met someone, so I'm gonna hang out with him. We can meet back at my place if you're cool with that."

I shook my head in disapproval, as she stumbled into the guy's direction. This was supposed to be *our* night out together.

Someone bumped into the back of my chair. Thinking it was Terese again, I jerked my head around. I was just about to yell "F- you!" when I noticed a handsome man.

"Hey, I'm really sorry—" he yelled over the blaring song. "Wait, I know you!"

I had no idea what he was talking about. *How could we know each other?* "I think you're mistaken, so have a nice night," I said, turning around to enjoy more popcorn. I don't like pick-up lines. The music was so loud it drummed in my chest.

After twenty minutes, I put on my coat and headed for the bathroom. I saw the same man standing near the wall across the dance floor. He was staring at me. I pretended not to notice, and turned the other way.

After I exited the bathroom, someone grabbed my hand. My body whirled around and I came face to face with that same man from earlier.

"I know you," he yelled.

Trying forcefully to pull my hand from his grip, he bent down, pulled me toward him, and kissed me. We did know each other. I had a flashback to last May when he kissed me passionately in the back of a restaurant.

"Allie, it's been—"

"What? I can't hear you! It's too loud in here," I yelled.

He grabbed me by the arm, and, willingly, I followed. It was chilly outside, but we ran to a nearby, heated gazebo. Once inside, he braced me against the wall, just like last time. With an aching desire, I wanted him again, more than before.

I ran my hand up his back and grabbed his head, pressing it in my direction until our lips forcibly met in another hot, passionate kiss. His hands worked their way up my sides and then back down, as if he was sanding my whole body. My head lay against his chest as he ran his fingers through my hair. Warm sensations ran through me. I wanted more but didn't know how to ask. His fingers found their way to my lips and into my mouth. I sensed his fervor, and, at that moment, I knew we were craving the same thing. Carefully, he lay my throbbing body on a cushioned bench, took off my pants, and unzipped his jeans. He felt warm as lava as his body hovered over mine, and we began to move in rhythm, as if dancing slowly to our own music. I felt attractive and protected, two feelings I wasn't sure I'd ever feel again.

☙ ❧

I rolled over on the bench at 2:00 a.m. Just like that, he was gone. When my eyes adjusted in the dark, I saw one fresh red rose, a fifty dollar bill and a note scribbled in ink.

Allie, you — we are amazing! Have to go. Will explain next time. Money for a cab. I hope we see each other again — Cole.

I turned the paper over, looking for more, just as I had done with the note Daniel left when he vanished. While Cole was just a fling, I began to develop feelings for this mystery man. I got dressed, walked into the cold wind, and flagged down a cab.

Inside the heated car, I daydreamed about our time together only a few hours ago. Warmth cradled my inner body as I thought about our passionate kisses and the moment our bodies became one. Elated, I wondered when I'd see him again.

The cab dropped me off at Terese's condo. Her door was open, and I walked in, half asleep. Everything was dark, so I went to bed, pulling the sheets over me to warm my body. As I thought about my night of passion with Cole, tingly sensations plucked my skin. I could still smell his cologne on my shirt, and I loved the way he held me in his secure embrace. I didn't want the night to end. I was still elated thinking about the man I had only been with a few times. Finally, I drifted to sleep.

The next morning, I decided to stay in bed for a while. The night before seemed like a dream, and I had a hard time believing I was in a gazebo in the middle of winter with a man I was slowly falling for. Even though we hadn't really talked, there was something about him I intuitively sensed. I felt like I'd known him for a long time.

My mind drifted back to Mom and the two letters I found at her gravesite. As I reflected on Cole and our times together, I thought about those letters.

Having spent last night with a wonderful man, I realized Mom may have loved someone like that. Just like Rose loved Ron, and Gracie loved Lance. It was all starting to make sense. True love is rare. Who am I to take that away from the most important woman in my life?

I walked into the living room still in my pajamas. Terese was sitting next to the sliding glass balcony door sipping coffee.

"Eh hem," I said, not wanting to startle her.

"Faith!" Terese set her coffee down, rose from her chair, and gave me a big hug. "I'm so sorry about our spat last night. Are you alright? What happened to you? I was so worried about you this morning."

"Hey, I'm alright. Well, actually, I met someone last night. I mean, I re-met someone last night." I giggled.

"Oh, really? You have to tell me," Terese begged.

"Oh, alright." I couldn't hold it in any longer, still feeling ecstatic about our night together. "The man from the first time we went out to Gaby's was the same man from last night. His name is Cole, and he has a way of sweeping me off my feet, quite literally. We've had two nights of passion so far, two incredibly delicious nights, if you know what I mean," I laughed, feeling like a teenager again. I didn't tell Terese that I kissed him at the Japanese restaurant during my last visit. I wanted to keep that a secret for now.

"Wow! That's really cool! So, what happened? Where's he now?" she asked, sipping her coffee.

"Well, when I woke up, he was gone. It's just my luck, isn't it, that men leave me?" But, I couldn't be mad at him.

"Wait, he left just like that? Did he say anything to indicate where he was going?"

"I was sleeping, remember? We didn't talk that much

'cause our lips were locked the entire time. I just remember cozying up to him and falling asleep. But . . ."

"But what? Oh, you gotta tell me what happened! I'm dying to know," Terese pleaded.

"He left me one fresh red rose, fifty dollars for a cab, and a note." I read the note to her.

"That's sweet, but what a jerk for leaving! Where did he have to go at 2:00 in the morning anyway? That bothers me. He's just playing you," she said angrily.

"We were both slightly buzzed, and truly, I wanted to have a few drinks and relax. I just didn't expect I would relax in *that* way." I was giggling again. It was embarrassing to talk in detail about my one-night stand. "And really, I don't live here anymore, so maybe it's better we don't know each other and that we have these occasional mysterious nights of passion when I come to New York City."

"Well, I sure as hell would be mad. But if you're not, that's good."

"I think I'm falling for him, even though I'll never see him again unless I come back here and go back to Gaby's, hoping he'll be there."

"Wow, really? After meeting him a couple times, that's how you feel?"

I nodded and continued, "I want to apologize to you for my behavior last night. I'm sorry I reacted that way when you asked me about my mom's letters. After I was with Cole, I realized that if Mom had a lover before she passed away, kudos to her. And I really want to read that other letter now. If anything, it will teach me more about her."

Terese nodded. "I'm glad you decided to read it. How exciting for you to unravel this mystery. You'll have to call and let me know what it says. I can't wait to hear from you again."

"Being with Cole makes me want to find my own lover. I think I'm ready, and if I wait much longer, I may be admitted into a nursing home." I giggled again, feeling satisfied from last night.

To celebrate the one-year anniversary of my move to Hill City, Terese and I went out to dinner at an Italian restaurant down the street. We talked and laughed all night.

Chapter 22

Once I arrived home in Hill City, I ran into the bedroom and threw my bags on the floor. After my wonderful steamy weekend away, I couldn't wait to read the remaining letter. I rummaged through the dresser drawer and found the plastic bag I had so carefully preserved it in. Gently I brought it into the living room. As I sat on the couch and held the letter tucked snug in the baggie, my heart pounded.

I opened the bag. The note was dirty and had water stains. Written in light pencil, it was hard to read. I found my magnifying glass, turned on the lamp, laid the note on the coffee table, and straightened out its creases. Oddly, this note wasn't addressed to anyone.

I thought about you today, as I do every day. You are so beautiful. My Angel has been sent from heaven. Love ...

My heart ached that this man got to know Mom while

I was preoccupied with Daniel, unable to remember her. I read the three sentences over and over. The paper smelled musty. I folded it up and put it away. *Are there any more letters?*

Sadly, no dates were on the two letters. It didn't matter anyway, since Mom was gone. *Who wrote these letters? Was he still in love with her?*

I hadn't talked about Mom with many people except for Gracie, Gayle, and Terese, and none of them mentioned a lover. Then again, no one mentioned Mom either until very recently.

It was a Monday in mid-January, and I didn't need to go back to work until later in the week. Terese was right. I was excited to see if there were more letters. After eating lunch, I went on my usual jog to go see Mom. It was sixty degrees, a warm winter in this part of the country. The possibility of finding more letters made me run faster.

When I arrived, I walked through the long grass to get to Mom's stone. Thoughts of her lover drifted into my mind. *Is he still alive? Does he live in Hill City? What if I could meet him?*

Pacing close to her stone and catching my breath, I said, "Hi, Mom. I'm back from my visit with Terese. Can you believe I've been here one year? I'm glad Terese steered me back to you. I love being here. It's peaceful and beautiful. The last time I was here, I found letters. I don't know who they're from, but I'm guessing your lover."

I dug in the sand close to her gravestone, but I didn't spot any pieces of paper sticking out of the ground. Disappointment crept into my heart. Just then, about a foot away from her stone, I saw something shiny and pink buried in the tall grasses. I walked over and knelt down, hoping it would be significant. I separated the delicate grasses with my fingers and pulled a piece of paper out from the ground. Like the others, it was dirty and stained.

"Oh wow, here's another one!" I gently opened it. Fortunately, it was written in black ink.

My Dear—I've been touched by an Angel, and my life now has meaning. You're my Angel and nothing will ever change that. Love...

The last note also said something about an Angel. *Was I too self-absorbed to notice these notes before? Were they here when I first visited Mom? Or have they recently been placed here?*

"So, who is he, Mom? I wish you were here, so you could tell me. Is he still alive? Was he a past lover?" It was pointless to focus on my questions. I wasn't going to get any answers.

I re-read the letter and tucked it away. "Mom, if you can hear me, please send me a sign. I love and miss you so much."

When I stood up to leave, an orange and black spotted monarch flew over to her stone and sat there, fluttering its wings.

As I jogged home, I thought about the new letter. I stopped at my favorite lookout, slowly pulled the note from my pocket, and read it again. Turning it over, I noticed something I hadn't seen before. There was the number four in the bottom right-hand corner, barely recognizable. *What's the significance of four? Is it the fourth day? Four o'clock? Maybe it's the fourth note?* Realizing this possibility, I dashed home.

Once there, my palms were sticky and wet. I went inside,

washed my hands, and carefully pulled out the other two letters. Under the lamp and with my magnifying glass, I turned each of them over and looked at the bottom right-hand corner. Sure enough, there were numbers two and three on the letters. That could only mean one thing. There were more to be found.

∽ ∾

On Tuesday, I couldn't wait to look for more letters. When I got to Mom's gravesite, I said, "Mom, I learned something about the letters, they're all numbered! I don't know how I missed that. This is like one big puzzle. I'll be here often, looking for more notes." I circled slowly around her headstone. My heart sank when I didn't see anything. I stopped. *Where would I hide letters?*

Crouching down, close to the sandy dirt, I saw a small piece of paper. It looked like an oversized gum wrapper. I picked it up and noticed it had writing. The words were too hard to read so I took my magnifying glass out of my pocket and read it aloud.

Dear You—I miss snuggling with you. I miss your scent, your motion, your rhythm. I miss feeling our bodies touch in the purest way and melting in your arms, hearing you breathe. Love...

I bellowed, "Oh. My. God. Mom—you were intimate with this guy?" I laughed nervously trying to lighten the flush of heat on my cheeks. "I don't need to know such details!" On the bottom corner, there was a number five.

So far, I had letters numbered two, three, four and five. Letter number one was missing. I feverishly looked around Mom's grave site, but came up empty-handed.

I pocketed the letter and ran home. I called St. Lucille's to ask for another day off. An employee I didn't know answered and said they didn't need me until Monday.

The next day, I awoke early. I gathered all the letters and read them again. They were written in the present tense, as if the man who had this undying love for mom was still here. I wanted to go back to look for missing letter number one.

∽ ∽

The bright sun pierced through the prickly pear cactus. The rays of light highlighted the red and pink desert hues. Towering green pine trees and majestic red canyons stood tall through all seasons in Arizona. A small, western banded gecko poked its head out from under a rock when I jogged by. Up ahead, a long slinky milk snake slithered across the path. I slowed down to a halt. *Ew, I hate snakes.* I jumped over it and ran far from that area.

When I arrived at the cemetery, I saw a shadow near Mom's stone. But as I got closer, it disappeared. *Could it be a spirit?* I shivered at the thought.

"Hi, Mom. I'm back to see you and find another letter. I think there are five in total." I walked around with my eyes closed, basking in the hot sun. I sat next to Mom and rocked back and forth. *How am I ever going to find one more letter?*

I picked up a large rock. Nothing was there but dirt. My heart sank. I spent a little more time sitting with Mom and then decided to go back home.

Later, I called Terese. "Hi, Terese," I said, trying to sound positive.

"Hey, Faith, nice to hear from you. Did you find any more letters?"

"Yes, I did, which is the reason I'm calling you."

"Oh, wow, this is my excitement for the week. Tell me more," she said, giggling.

"After I left you, I found two more letters, and guess what?" Before she could answer, I yelled, "They are all numbered!"

"Wow. What does that mean?" Terese asked.

"Well, I found letters numbered two, three, four, and five. So, I know there's at least one more letter to be found," I said eagerly.

"Awesome, where do you think it is?"

"I don't know, I didn't find any more letters today, so I'm not sure," I said, remembering my disappointment from earlier.

"I hope you find one soon! You'll have to read them to me another time. I have to run to an appointment. Let's talk soon." Terese said.

Chapter 23

In Hill City, the letters were my secret. I didn't want a lot of attention drawn to them—people speculating and getting into my business.

I went to see Mom two more times before I had to go back to work. There should've been at least one more letter, but I couldn't find it.

At work, I checked in with the residents, but many were napping, so it was a quiet day. This gave me time to think. *Where was that first letter?*

"Hi, Faith, what's wrong? Cat got your tongue?" Gayle asked.

"Hi." I didn't want to lie. "Just thinking is all."

Gayle was in a hurry. She walked past me and smiled.

Later, after my shift ended, I took a detour and visited Mom's grave. Since the letters started there, I needed to sort out my thoughts.

I sat by her stone, and spoke to her again. "Hi, Mom. I've come back. There's at least one more letter. I don't know where it is. I've scoured this place. Not knowing who wrote these letters is driving me crazy. I wish you were here, so you could tell me about your secret lover."

Just then, a golden retriever puppy bounced over to me. His tail wagged rapidly, and he jumped on me.

"Hi there, pup. What are you doing out here all alone?" I petted him, feeling his velvety fur between my fingertips.

Once the pup smelled and licked me all over, he walked over to Mom and started pawing at her stone. It was the cutest thing. Then five feet away, he began digging like adult dogs do when they're trying to bury a bone. He stopped to smell something and began digging again. I watched him in adoration. Still, there was not a soul in sight to claim him.

"Come here, boy." The puppy paid no attention to me and continued digging.

As I listened to his scratching a few feet away, I closed my eyes and soaked up the warm sun. A high-pitched whistle interrupted my thoughts. The puppy's dirty face rose from the ground. Its ears perked up. He ran off, toward the sound of the whistle, which came from behind the towering pine trees past Mom's gravestone.

"That was strange, but he was the cutest, wasn't he, Mom? I love dogs. Maybe I should get a puppy to keep me company now that I'm starting to feel like myself again. The only thing is, my memory isn't that good yet." I glanced over to where the puppy was digging and saw something. *Could it be? Another letter?*

I jumped up and sprinted over to the spot. Sure enough, there was paper wedged into the dirt.

The thing was caked with so much dirt that, for a moment, I thought it was food stuck to a wrapper. Inspecting it, my heart beat fast. *Is this the missing letter?*

Finding Faith

I couldn't make out anything on the paper, so I put it in my pocket.

"See you later, Mom. Looks like all I needed was a little puppy luck to help me find this." I giggled and ran home.

When I got there, I turned on the lamp and found my magnifying glass. A damp cloth helped peel away some of the dirt. Very carefully, I straightened out the edges and smoothed the surface of the paper. I gently washed away some of the soil that was crusted on the note. The whole thing dripped with water. I placed it on top of the table to dry and went to heat up some soup for a mid-afternoon snack, wondering whether the letter could be salvaged.

After twenty minutes of staring at the paper from across the room and wondering about all the letters, I walked over to it. I picked it up from the corner and put it under the lamp. I still couldn't make out what it said. Turning it over, I saw no number. The water-stained, dirty color was permanent. *Now what? This must be the missing letter, but it's ruined!*

∽ ∾

The next day, with a heavy heart, I went to St. Lucille's to talk with Gayle about the letters. When I arrived, she was checking the toiletry count in the closet.

"Hi, Gayle. I need to talk to you about something."

"Oh, good morning, Faith. It's nice to see you. What's up?" She looked at me briefly and then resumed rummaging through the items making a lot of noise.

"Can we go somewhere to talk?"

"Hang on. I just need to take down some numbers. I'll meet you in my office in ten minutes."

I went to her office and waited.

"Hey, Faith," Gayle sang, walking into her office. She sat on a brown plaid chair next to me. "Are you alright?"

I didn't know how to start the conversation. "I have a secret, and I need some help."

"Oh?" Gayle looked at me with raised eyebrows.

"I recently learned my mom lived and died here. It's a long story but I've been finding numbered letters by her grave. I don't know who they're from. Yesterday, I think I found another one. When I brought it home, it was too damaged to read and—"

"Hang on just a minute," Gayle stood up and walked out of her office. She reappeared with an envelope and handed it to me.

"What's this?"

"Well, it looks like an envelope," Gayle teased. "I'll tell you something. After your mom passed, a man walked in here and handed us this letter. His name was Michael. I was waiting until the right time to give this to you," she winked.

I grabbed it from her hand. "Oh my." *Is this the missing letter? Was Michael her lover?*

I fanned myself with the envelope. Thrilled and anxious, I got up from the chair and started pacing as I thought about all the possibilities.

"Sounds like you have some noodling to do. Why don't you take a few days off? When you're ready to come back to work again, let me know. We're not all that busy right now, so take as much time as you need." Gayle patted me on the shoulder and buzzed out of the room.

∽ ∾

At home, I carefully opened the envelope and read the most beautiful message.

Dear Angel—I remember waking up next to you that one morning. How beautiful you looked, sleeping peacefully. I've missed you every day since. Knowing you for only a short time has heightened my desire to touch you again. Time and distance will not change the way I hold you in my heart. You've opened me up in ways that I could never imagine. In your memory, I'll be gazing out our window at Café Amor in Sedona on Friday at 6:00 pm. You have been a part of me for so long, let me be a part of you. Come find me. All my love . . .

I read the letter over and over, wondering about Michael. I turned over the piece of paper and found a number six on the bottom right-hand corner. The letter was out of sequence, and I was wrong. There were six letters.

Then it hit me; he's still alive!

Chapter 24

I borrowed Gayle's car on Friday night. I didn't know how to get to Café Amor in Sedona, but Gayle provided me with a map. A few times during the trip, my left leg bounced nonstop. A headache was looming, and my jaw clenched. I almost didn't go.

I followed Gayle's directions and came to a fork in the road. To the left, there were lots of cacti and plants standing in the desert sand, and to the right, there was a tall lit sign that read Café Amor. It was 5:30 p.m. I was thirty minutes early.

I decided to drive around the area. Colored canyons jetted out from the earth. Tall, prickly cacti stood unwavering in the light breeze. Sand coated the ground, and I smelled a mix of sage and dust in the mild air.

I parked on a side road and turned off the engine. Stillness. A part of me wanted time to freeze so I could be stuck here. A bigger part of me wondered who Michael was and how he fit into Mom's life.

I looked at my watch. I still had twenty minutes before I had to go back to the café. I propped my chin on my hands, leaned on the steering wheel and looked out at God's Country.

I closed my eyes and breathed deeply, trying to calm my nerves that lit up under my skin. Soon I melted into a tranquil state of mind.

A while later, I opened my eyes. It was one minute past 6:00 p.m.. I gasped. I started the car and the engine roared as I drove off.

When I pulled into the parking lot, the jitters quickly returned. I got out of the car and looked up at the full moon. I felt small compared to its majesty.

The café was surrounded by giant pieces of sharp, pointed, red rocks. All sizes of cacti with white and yellow flowers dotted the grounds. A brook babbled nearby. A coyote howled in the distance and sent shivers up my spine.

I walked up to the café and opened the door. A quiet chatter filled my ears. Luckily, the place was a bar, and I didn't need to face embarrassment of being there alone. I sat at a high-top table and slowly scanned the area.

My eyes fixated on a gentleman looking out a tall window that overlooked the moonlit peaks of rock. I couldn't see his face.

"Hi there, welcome to Café Amor." A high-pitched woman's voice distracted me. "May I get you something to eat or drink?" The waitress smiled coyly.

Caught off guard, I said, "Yes, I'll have a beer." I continued admiring the man near the window.

"Alright, well, what kind of beer, on tap or—"

"Yes, sure, on tap, whatever you recommend." She was in my way.

Her smile quickly disappeared. She strolled over to the bar to get my beer.

I looked for the man near the window, but he was gone. *Oh no!*

The waitress reappeared with my beer. I thanked her kindly, told her I wasn't staying long, and paid my bill.

I heard a soft voice in my mind urging me to wait awhile. I exhaled a heavy breath of impatient air.

I remembered that the letters brought me here. I sat back in the chair, trying to relax, and took a few sips of my beer. I thought about the five letters that were now in my possession. One was still missing. *What do they mean? Why were they buried near Mom's gravesite? Will I get to meet her mystery lover tonight?*

I drank the beer too fast and felt lightheaded. I spotted some popcorn and walked over to get a basket. Eating something settled my stomach. *There has to be a message in those letters.*

All of a sudden, something dawned on me. The sixth letter, the whole reason I'm at this café tonight . . . *Wait a minute. Oh my God! How could I be so dumb?*

I was so consumed by these mysterious letters that all common sense flew out the window.

The fifth letter. I received it two days ago, but it was given to Gayle right after mom died. What was I thinking? *I'm a year too late!*

My heart sank and tears welled up in my eyes.

Before I left Café Amor, I sulked over to the large window to see what Mom saw when she was alive. It was amazing! A tunnel of moonlight glowed through ponderosa pines and their shadows came alive in the evening breeze.

I felt Mom again. Through watery eyes, I took one final look to engrave this sight into my memory.

As I turned around, I bumped into someone. I looked up and gasped. It was Cole.

Chapter 25

"What, how, where . . ." Words fumbled from my lips. *What's he doing here?* I had a flashback of us making love.

"Well, hello, Allie. Fancy seeing you in this neck of the woods," he said, backing up a few steps.

Not knowing what to say, I stood there, speechless. *Should I continue the lie about my name or tell the truth?*

"Well, you're the last person I expected to see here. Don't we normally meet up in New York City?" I tried to laugh.

"Who were you expecting to see?" His eyes searched mine.

"Not you," I quietly mumbled. "So, why are you here?" There was so much I didn't know about Cole.

"I'm traveling for business. I love this part of the country; it's so beautiful. What brings you to Sedona?"

In an attempt to avoid conversation, I walked toward

the table. Leaning against a chair, I grabbed my beer and rerouted the conversation.

"I still don't get why you're *here*," I said, looking up into his dreamy eyes.

I remembered kissing him in the gazebo. The thought of his body pulsating on top of mine made my face flush.

"Okay, okay. I've waited long enough. Allie, I knew your mom and—"

What? My heart fell and feelings of sadness and anger came flooding back. "Wait, what? You knew my mom too? How many other people knew my mom? What is this, some kind of joke? I don't know who you are, where you're from or the reason we keep running into each other, but tonight you've gone too far! You know nothing about me!" My eyes teared.

Turning around, I walked quickly towards the exit. I flung the door open and the air dried my face.

"Wait! Allie, wait!"

I stopped, unable to move. Cole ran up to me, grabbed my arm and whipped me around to face him. Instantly, I felt his hold. His hands cupped my head, and our eyes met.

"I just gotta do this." Cole's lips covered mine. Heat spread through my veins, and in a second, I was back at the gazebo, the sexual tension bubbling.

My mind snapped into focus.

"I need to go! I can't do this anymore. Please stop following me, and leave me alone!" I broke away from his grip and ran to my car.

"Wait, Allie! If you don't believe me, read the note I left you in the gazebo. I . . ."

Barely hearing him, I opened the car door and jumped inside. Turning the key, I drove off.

Tears streamed down my face. *Did that really happen?*

Somehow, I made it home even though I was fuming. Once inside, I slammed my body onto the bed and sobbed. *Who does he think he is saying he knew Mom? He knows nothing about me!* I cried, eventually falling asleep.

I woke up early the next morning, remembering the night before, which felt like a dream. I lay in bed. *How in the world would Cole know about Mom? Why would he say such a thing, without ever talking to me? He doesn't even know me.*

I didn't see Michael at Café Amor. That halted the mystery behind the letters. I never imagined I would run into Cole here, in Arizona. When he said he knew Mom, I felt like someone had stabbed me in the heart. All the sadness and anger I felt when Gracie told me about Mom returned.

Suddenly, I remembered pieces of what Cole said. I jumped out of bed and rummaged through the dresser drawers until I found the note Cole left for me at the gazebo.

Allie, you—we were amazing! Have to go. Will explain next time. Money for a cab. I hope we see each other again—Cole.

I read it again, recalling our final night together. The line *will explain next time,* stung. I flipped the paper over. The number one was written in the bottom right corner. The sequence was complete.

Chapter 26

The next day, I ran to Gracie's house. Because she had been Mom's close friend, maybe she'd know something about these letters and this Michael character. Feverishly, I pounded on her door.

"Just a minute," she yelled.

Gracie opened the door and smiled when she saw me. "Oh, hello, Faith. This is a nice surprise. Do come in."

"Hi. I need to talk with you about something." As we hugged, my heart pounded in my chest.

"Let's sit down. I've just made tea. Would you care for a cup?" When I nodded, she shuffled over to the kitchen to get me a cup of tea.

"I don't know what I've told you about my visits to see Mom, but I've found these letters at her gravesite, and I think they're from someone special Mom knew when she was still alive. It could've been someone who liked her. I'm not really sure but . . ."

"Hold on. Let me get this straight. You found letters at your mother's gravesite?" Gracie raised her eyebrows and looked confused.

"Yep. The letters are numbered. Over several visits, I found letters two through five. Then, last week, I asked Gayle if she knew anything about these letters, and she gave me a note from a man named Michael who brought it to St. Lucille's after Mom died. I don't know who he is, but the number six was on the back of that letter." I paused to drink some tea and catch my breath.

"Hmm . . ." Gracie looked up at the ceiling and appeared deep in thought.

"Do you have any idea about the letters or who this Michael guy is?" I asked.

"No, but something your mom said is starting to make some sense."

"Oh my goodness, what is it?" My heart beat faster. "I need to know. Please, tell me." I leaned forward and took another sip of tea.

"Before your mom died, she told me she was leaving something for you." She got up to fill our cups with more tea.

"But what does that mean? It could be anything. And how would she know about the letters?"

"Perhaps you're not meant to know now. The answer will come in time," Gracie said confidently.

My body temperature climbed. *Why isn't anyone being upfront with me? Don't they get how important this is to me?*

Feeling a need to leave, something I do when I'm upset, I rose to my feet. "Okay, I'll think about what you said. I better get going. I need to go home to re-read the letters."

Instead of going home, I headed into town to see Gayle.

By the time I arrived at St. Lucille's, my body temperature was back to normal. *Obviously, there's a reason for these letters, and Gayle will tell me.*

Leo was at the front desk, his back to me. "Hey, Leo, do you know where I can find Gayle?"

He jumped and turned around. "Hi, Faith. You have a knack for startling me. You almost missed her. She's here, but leaving soon. Her shift just ended." He motioned for me to go to her office.

I knocked on her door and gently pushed it open.

Gayle looked up and smiled. "Hey, Faith! How are you?"

"Hi, Gayle. I could be better." I took a seat in front of her desk.

"Do tell. Did you find Café Amor the other night?" she asked, putting down the stack of papers she was reading.

"Yes, I did. Thanks for the directions. It was a waste of time." I looked past her and out the window, remembering the emotional night.

"I'm sorry to hear that. Tell me what happened." She scooted her chair closer to the desk and looked at me.

"It's a long story. The letter said that Michael would be at Café Amor. I was so excited to meet him. Then it dawned on me that—"

"You were too late," Gayle said, putting the pieces together.

"Yes, that's right. I was too late." My heart felt heavy again.

"Oh, I'm sorry." Gayle rose from her chair and walked over to give me a hug. "I'm so sorry."

"There's more," I said.

"Oh?" She sat down, and studied me.

"Before I left the café, I ran into someone I wasn't expecting to see. Someone I met in New York City. The last time I saw him, he left me a note. Last night, he told me to read that note again, so I read it today and there was a number on the right corner, completing my sequence of letters. I don't know if it's a coincidence, but his name is Cole, not Michael, so I have no new information about Michael. The man who wrote Mom that letter you gave me, wasn't at Café Amor." I let out a deep sigh.

"Wow, that's quite the story." Gayle leaned back in her chair and crossed her legs. "Unfortunately, all I know is that Michael was a special visitor who came to see your mom. I started working here shortly before your mom died, so I don't know the full story, but I vaguely remember he was a handsome gentleman. I'm sorry to say I have no other information about him," she said, with sad eyes and a half frown.

I got up from the chair and gave her a hug. "Thanks for listening and for telling me this. I'll keep you posted if anything else happens, which is highly doubtful."

I walked out of the room and headed home; my head hung low.

When I got home, I ate lunch and changed into something more comfortable. By mid-afternoon, I decided to go back to the cemetery.

On my way into the desert valley, my mind felt like one big jigsaw puzzle. I jogged toward the cemetery to clear my head.

The sky was bright blue. The sun's rays glided over the mountain peaks. It was a warm and clear day with no wind.

Once at the gate to the cemetery, I walked around in

circles to catch my breath before going to Mom's gravesite. I was hoping to find answers about Michael and his letters. This was the last place I would try.

Out of nowhere, the golden retriever puppy returned. I kneeled down to pet him.

"Hi there, pup. You're back and just as cute!" I looked up, but I saw no one. I turned my attention back to the small ball of fur. "Where's your owner?"

Just then, I heard that piercing whistle. The pup's ears perked up. This time he stayed put and barked. When he saw someone walk out of the woods by Mom's stone, he stopped barking. The puppy continued wagging its tail, licking, and jumping on me. I giggled at how playful he was.

"Hal! Come here, boy!" A man's booming voice called out in our direction.

The puppy stopped and looked toward the sound. Then, he ran in circles around me, jumping into the air. I laughed.

A man sprinted in our direction. Captivated by the puppy, I hardly noticed when he approached us.

"Hal!" An exasperated voice yelled. The puppy ran over to him.

I looked up, but the sun blocked my view. I stood up and moved away from the sun's glare. As my eyes adjusted, my jaw dropped. Standing there with the puppy was Cole.

What the heck? I blinked and rubbed my eyes, as if they were playing tricks on me. I took another look.

"Again! What are you doing here?" I asked. Surprisingly, butterflies stirred in my stomach. The sun hit his hair just right and it looked like there was a halo over his head.

"Allie? Fancy running into you in a cemetery of all places," he smiled, winking at me.

Fighting the urge to stare at this handsome man, I scowled. *Why is he here? Is this his puppy? And who is Hal? The dog?*

My hand swept over my head. Wisps of hair hung in strands outside my ponytail and sweat dripped down the side of my face. Quickly, I wiped my face with my sleeve.

"Yes, fancy that," I whispered, suddenly feeling self-conscious.

"What?" Cole walked a few steps closer to me with a big smirk on his face.

"I don't understand why you're here. And, why were you at the café last night? You said it was for business, but now you appear to have a dog."

"Allie, I need to tell you something." Cole's face grew serious.

My heart raced. Just then, the weather changed. The air cooled, and clouds rolled through the sky, threatening rain. I still hadn't seen Mom.

"I think it's gonna rain. I need to go before I get soaking wet." I zipped up my sweater and began jogging away from him.

I looked behind me and saw Cole standing there with the puppy at his side. Almost immediately, the wind picked up, and droplets of rain splashed on my head. As I sprinted across the cemetery and onto the path that would bring me home, the raindrops got bigger and stronger. Thunder echoed in the distance. *The last thing I need is to get hit by lightning!* My safety was more important than listening to his confession.

At the same time, a small part of me remembered the last time we were together and the passion we experienced.

I still felt his soft, warm lips kissing mine. The trouble was, I thought I'd never see him again.

I approached the lookout where I usually met up with Gracie and heard a loud voice boom across the sounds of rain and thunder.

"Allieeee, waaaait up!"

I looked back and saw Cole running toward me. He was carrying the puppy.

Confused, I froze while the rain pounded my body.

Cole stopped running when he got closer to me. Through the noise of the wind and rain, he yelled, "Allie, I need—tell—something!"

"Can't this wait? It's raining! I need to go," I screamed back.

"But, it's important!" He walked closer to me.

The rain came down in a torrent. It pounded on the ground, and dirt splashed on my legs.

"I'm sorry, but I really need to—"

"Allie, please, listen to me," he shouted.

I glanced at the sky, turned around, and ran as fast as I could.

When I got home, the rain was coming down so fast I couldn't see the lock on the door. As I fumbled for the key in my wet pocket, I heard a dog bark. I turned around. *How dare he follow me here?*

Cole stood there in the rain, ten steps in front of my house. He put the puppy down and it ran over to me. I quickly unlocked the door so he could run inside and seek shelter, something I should've been doing.

When I turned around, I saw fierce raindrops pelting Cole's skin.

"Allie—I have to talk to you," Cole yelled through the thunderstorm, taking two steps forward.

"I have to go! I can't do this now! If you haven't noticed, it's raining!"

"Damn it, Allie! Just listen to me!"

Something in his voice stopped me in my tracks. I froze. I was shivering as I stood on the porch. The rain, combined with thundering skies, was deafening.

Cole hollered, "I've waited too long for you!"

"What are you talking about? You know nothing about me! Plus, every time we see each other, you leave!" I was soaking wet and got more upset as I watched him walk toward me.

Heavy wet strands of hair coated my head. Even under the roof, the wind whipped all around me. My shoes were flooded in water that had collected on the porch.

"You're wrong! I know more about you than you think! I never wanted to leave you, but I had to!"

The thunder and rain became louder. Even though I saw Cole's lips moving I could barely make out what he was saying.

"I—into you—the store—Hill City!"

This wasn't making sense.

"I love you, Allie!"

Time stopped. *What?* Rain continued to bombard me, yet I froze as an ocean of anger rushed forward, flashing me back to my painful breakup with Daniel. *Daniel said he loved me and then he left me! After Cole and I made love, he left me too! How could he love me? He doesn't even know me!*

I stomped down the porch steps and into the rain towards Cole, "No, no, no! You don't love me; that's impossible!

You don't even know me! I don't know what you want from me, but you need to leave right *now*!" Tears stung my eyes.

Lightning lit the sky, immediately followed by a loud clatter of thunder. We jumped.

Cole grabbed my body.

"Get your hands off me!"

With all his strength, he pulled me through the wind and rain onto the porch, out of harm's way.

"What are you doing? Let me go," I cried.

Cole grabbed my head and kissed me so hard that I almost fell over. Feeling his lips on mine, I crumbled. I kissed him back, my face mixed with tears and rain.

As Cole wrapped his arms around my body, I pushed the door open. A clap of thunder roared through the house and lightning lit up the living room. Then, everything went dark.

Suddenly, I wasn't angry anymore. I wanted him more than ever. Once we were inside the house, he pressed me against the wall, and kissed me.

"I've missed you so much," he murmured in a seductive tone. Cole's tongue familiarized itself with the inside of my mouth.

We moved from the wall to my bedroom, our lips still locked together. There, in the darkness, he took off his shirt and pulled down his pants. His heavy breathing was inches from my ear. He gently unzipped my sweater and took it off, along with my shirt. Then, he peeled off my pants. The air dried our bodies as Cole lay me on the bed and carefully got on top of me, pressing his hardness into me.

Cole kissed me all over, while his warm, muscular hands caressed my being. The thunder rattled forcibly outside and, knowing we were safe inside, intensified my craving for him. I shifted my body to meet his. Groaning with deep pleasure, he slid into me again as the thunder cracked louder than before. We held onto each other fiercely and he rocked me hard and long until we both reached ecstasy. Afterwards, Cole lay next to me, cradling me in his arms and we fell asleep to the sound of the then quiet rain.

The next morning, I opened my eyes and saw the sun shining in through the window. I rolled over, expecting to see Cole, but he was gone. Instead, there was a note on the pillow.

Allie, I missed having Faith. But then you came into my life. Last night was beautiful and magical. I hope to see you soon.
Cole

Just then, Hal ran into my bedroom, jumped on the bed, and started licking my face.

Chapter 27

I remembered the night of passion and smiled, feeling warm vibrations float over my naked body. Cole's note mentioned my real name. This could only mean one thing. He had answers.

I took a shower, got dressed, and walked into the kitchen with Hal at my feet.

"You must be hungry," I said as I poured some water into a bowl and placed it on the floor. He slurped it all up. I looked around for something a puppy could eat and found a small package of dog food on the counter. Cole must've left it. I poured the food into another bowl and put it on the floor next to the water bowl. Hal eagerly licked the bowl clean.

I ate an apple and made some toast. As I sat down at the table to eat, I wondered how I would find Cole. Hal wasn't wearing a collar with a dog tag, but I had an idea. After breakfast, I grabbed my keys, jacket and whistled for Hal to come outside.

"So, where do we find your papa?"

Hal looked up at me tilting his head, as if he was trying to understand what I was saying. Suddenly, we heard sirens in the distance and he took off running. I sprinted after him.

Every once in a while, Hal would glance back at me, his tongue dangling out of his mouth, making sure I was still hot on his trail. I never heard sirens in Hill City and I wondered why Hal was running in that direction.

When we got to Betty's Restaurant, he stopped. Smoke was billowing from the rooftop, and there were flames.

"Oh, my," I gasped in shock.

There was a buzz of people gathered in the area as well as a medium-sized fire truck. Firefighters climbed the fully extended ladder and sprayed water, which added to the stifling smoke. I backed up, coughing. Hal barked and cried.

"Come here, boy." I knelt down and extended my arms. Hal turned around and walked over to me, seeming comforted that I was paying attention to him in the midst of all this fury.

I hadn't seen a real fire before and I was worried. There were onlookers near the charred restaurant, but I didn't recognize anyone. I petted Hal to calm him. *How did the fire start? Is anyone hurt?*

A fireman sauntered over to us. He looked at me and tipped his hat in a silent hello and bent down to pet the dog. "Hey Hal, buddy," he said.

Surprised, I started to ask who he was when he spoke into his radio, "They're here and fine, Jake. I'm coming!" He stood up and ran toward the restaurant.

Hal stopped barking, jumped on me, and licked my face.

"Woah, buddy," I said, surprised by his sudden change in demeanor.

"Hal!"

Hal ran. I looked up and saw another man, dressed head to toe in a fire suit, complete with a gas mask. He picked up Hal and walked over to me.

I stood up and straightened my shirt. It wasn't every day I met a fireman.

He approached me and I smiled. I couldn't see his eyes.

"Hi, gorgeous," he echoed through the mask.

My eyes widened. "Do I know you?"

"I'm Jake," he said.

"Jake who?" I was so confused.

He unsnapped his mask and took it off. Dark ash covered his face, yet his piercing blue eyes looked right through me. He looked familiar, but so did many people.

"Jake, as in me, Cole." He laughed and reached for my hand.

"Huh?" My mouth opened wide. My eyebrows raised. He had a flair for showing up at the most inopportune times.

His fingers webbed into mine and I knew right away it was Cole. Hours before, we lay coiled together. I would never forget his touch.

"Why are you dressed up as a fireman?" I wasn't thinking.

"Because I volunteer with the fire department," he chuckled, squinting at me through the sunlight.

"*What?*" I stepped back and studied him. I couldn't take my eyes off him.

"I'll explain later." Cole pulled me toward him and stared deep into my eyes.

He looked terribly tired. Suddenly, he started coughing.

"Oh my goodness, are you alright? What can I do? Is there anything I can do?"

Cole didn't respond, so I called for help.

A couple of firemen rushed over and laid him on the ground. They grabbed his gas mask, put it on his mouth and turned on a gadget that pumped clean air into it.

I looked at him and it dawned on me that he had been fighting a real fire. I was afraid he might be seriously injured. I lost Mom already. I wasn't about to lose Cole.

Chapter 28

"Back up, everyone, the man needs space! Back up!" A fireman was tending to Cole.

By this time, people were all around him. Reluctantly, I followed the order to step back.

My heart pounded. Hal tried to get to Cole, but I squatted down and held onto him. At first, I thought Cole was choking, but the firemen protected their partner and hovered over him like it was much worse.

I saw Cole's arms and legs lying on the ground, but he wasn't moving. I had no information about what was going on, so I kept quiet in a slow panic.

An ambulance rolled onto the scene and stopped a few feet from Cole. The firefighters lifted him onto a stretcher, put him in the back of the truck, and quickly closed the door.

Although I wanted to be with him, I had no choice but to spin around and head home with Hal.

The back door of the ambulance flew open. "Wait! Wait! Is there an Allie in the crowd?" a medic yelled.

My heart stopped.

I turned around and ran toward the ambulance with Hal. One of the firefighters swept Hal up into his arms. He whined and cried as I jumped into the ambulance.

"Ma'am, Jake was asking for you. I hope it's okay if we take you with us." He pointed to a place for me to sit next to Cole and slammed the door shut.

"Of course," I said, thankful to be close to him.

Cole's eyes were closed and he was breathing into a machine, much like some of the residents at St. Lucille's.

I found his hand and cupped it in mine, holding onto it. "What happened to him?" I asked.

"Jake here, he got really close to the fire. Smoke inhalation. It's real bad for the body. We need to take him in to make sure he's okay," the medic said.

"Jake?" I asked, confused by the wrong name.

"Jake is a name a fire department gives to a hero on their team."

"Oh," I said, wondering what he had done to earn his heroism.

All the way to the clinic, I stared at Cole. I knew so little about him. I didn't know why Cole was working with the local fire department while his home was in New York City.

After twenty minutes, the ambulance pulled to a stop. The back doors swung open and a bunch of medics got Cole out of the truck.

I hopped out of the van and followed them into the hospital.

"You need to wait there, Allie," one of the medics said,

as she pointed to the waiting area. "Someone will come and get you when it's okay to see him."

I nodded reluctantly. All I wanted was to be with Cole. I walked to the waiting area at the other end of the hall and sat in one of the purple circular chairs. The TV was blaring in the background, which wasn't helping my looming headache. I hadn't eaten lunch yet.

I closed my eyes and rested my head on my hand. My heart was still pounding in my chest. Finally, the noise began to fade away.

"Miss? Miss?" A young doctor stood in front of me.

I jumped and stood up. "Yes? What's wrong? How's Cole?"

"I didn't mean to startle you, I'm Doctor Godfrey," she said.

She looked like she was twenty years old. She was stunning with dark black, shoulder length hair and green eyes. She was calm, which sent waves of peace through my body.

"Cole is asking to see you, but please keep in mind that he has been through a lot. He came very close to the fire and inhaled a great deal of smoke. He's still weak and tired."

I nodded, trying to process what she was saying. She motioned me to follow her. When we got to Cole's room, she nudged me to go in.

This was the first time I'd seen someone behind closed doors in a hospital. My heart jumped into a fast rhythm as I quietly walked into the room.

Cole was lying in bed, his face clean and his eyes shut. I cleared my throat to let him know I was near. He didn't move.

I sat down next to the hospital bed and picked up his

rugged, strong hand. Instantly, electrical currents ran from his fingers into mine.

"Hi, Cole, I'm here." I had a chilling déjà vu feeling, something I'd experienced with Mom at the cemetery when I first talked with her.

I sat back in the chair and stared at him. This was one of the first times I'd seen him in the light. He was strikingly handsome, with dark blonde hair and fair skin. I saw his muscular silhouette as he lay under the covers.

I knew nothing about this man except how I felt the handful of times I lay underneath his body. *I want to know everything about you.*

I was getting drowsy, so I bowed my head and closed my eyes.

"Ali . . ." A muffled voice startled me.

My head jolted up. Cole's lips were trying to move. I squeezed his hand and felt him clutch mine.

"Cole, I'm here," I said looking into his eyes.

He formed a soft smile. "Thanks for being here," he said, licking his lips.

I saw a cup of water with a straw on the table next to his bed. I reached for it and held the straw to his lips. He looked deeply into my eyes as if to say something, and then he sipped the water until it was gone.

"I was so thirsty," he murmured.

"Cole, is there anyone in your family I can call?"

He shook his head and looked away. "Both of my parents passed away and I'm an only child."

"Oh, I'm so sorry."

"It's okay," Cole said, his eyes looking at mine again.

"Are you able to talk or do you want to rest?"

"We can talk a little," he said.

"I hate seeing you like this, but I'm glad to be here with you. I was so scared when I saw you at Betty's." I fidgeted in my seat remembering that sight only a couple hours ago.

"Betty and I go way back. I worked at Betty's when I lived in Hill City a long time ago."

"You used to live in Hill City? When was that?"

Cole began to cough.

"Don't worry. We don't need to talk about it now. I just want you to get better." I got up to fetch another cup of water from the sink.

Cole took a few more sips from the straw.

"I want to take you out on a real date," he said.

"I'd love that," I said, smiling at him.

Chapter 29

A week later, I found a note in my mailbox. Cole asked me to meet him for a picnic lunch at the same place Gracie took me to tell me about Mom.

On the way there, I remembered the last time I saw Cole. He was lying in the hospital room. I still didn't know why Cole was in Arizona.

When I got to the lookout, Cole was nowhere in sight. The pace looked deserted. Even his puppy Hal wasn't around. I froze, not knowing what to do. *Did I read the note right? Is it the right day? He did say today, didn't he? Where is . . . ?*

Just then, two muscular arms circled my body. I jumped and smiled, hoping it was Cole.

"Hi, gorgeous," he whispered in my ear. "I've missed you."

I turned to face him. Before I could say anything, Cole's lips found mine, and we kissed deeply.

"You're here after all," I gasped.

"You didn't think I'd miss this, did you? I would've climbed over mountains to be here with you." He kissed my ear lobe, which sent shivers down my neck, and stirred me up inside.

I closed my eyes as his soft lips met mine again, continuing our kiss. Cole's hands hugged me tightly as he pushed his body into mine. We both moaned.

Lost in the moment, I jolted forward when he stopped kissing me.

"I'd love to kiss you all day, but I have more planned for us today. Don't worry, we'll kiss again and again, but for now, come this way," Cole said, tenderly taking my hand.

"Oh, alright," I sighed.

Cole led me into a canyon I never knew existed. A blue plaid blanket, a picnic basket, and a bottle of Pinot Noir were laid out on the ground.

"Wow, is this for me?" I teased.

"Of course," he smiled.

Kneeling down on the blanket, I reached for the wine.

"Where's Hal?" I asked.

"I left him home with some friends."

"Home? Where do you live? There's so much I don't know about you."

"That's why I invited you here today. So, we can get to know each other, face-to-face, instead of body-to-body," Cole laughed.

I handed him the bottle of wine and he poured two glasses. He opened the picnic basket and handed me a sandwich, a bag of Sunchips, and a Honey Crisp apple.

"Thanks," I beamed.

"I can cook, but today, I just threw this together so we can focus on getting to know each other. To us, and to learning about each other the right way," Cole said. We clinked our wine glasses.

I bit into my sandwich. "How did you know turkey and cheese is my favorite sandwich? It's delicious."

"It's my favorite, too," Cole said, opening his bag of chips.

"I'm so hungry," I said, biting into my sweet apple.

Cole smiled. "Thank you for meeting with me today. It meant a lot that you were at the hospital last week."

"I was glad to be there. How are you feeling? What happened?"

Cole looked at me. "I'm better. Much better. I got too close to the fire and inhaled too much smoke."

"Yeah, just don't do that again. I was really worried about you and I can't imagine what I'd do if anything worse happened to you." A chip crackled in my mouth, and I savored the salty taste.

"So, why do the firemen call you Jake? One of the medics in the ambulance said that name refers to someone who's a hero."

"Ah, yes, the notorious hero. I didn't think it was a big deal, but they consider me a hero because I saved myself." He took another bite of his sandwich and waited for my reaction.

"Saved yourself? Don't firefighters usually save other people?"

"Yes, they do. But in this situation, I was the one who needed to be saved. This will make more sense later, but before I joined the fire department, I was a mess. I was grieving so severely that I almost ended my own life. They consider me a hero because I enlisted in the fire department, which saved me. Helping other people helped me climb out of the funk I was in. Once the guys heard my story, they started calling me Jake. Kinda lame, know."

"Thank goodness you found a different way to deal with your pain. So, why did you want to meet here?"

"One reason I was in the cemetery the other week was to visit my parents who are buried there. When I come here, I can look out in that direction and feel them with me." He pointed to the cemetery with his glass and took a sip of wine.

Wow, this man is deep. "I'm sorry to hear about your parents. At the hospital you said you grew up here." I wanted to know all about this man.

"I miss my folks every day. And yep, I grew up in Hill City. Why were you in the cemetery that day?" Cole asked.

"My mom is buried there. It's a long story, but that's why I go there often." I squinted at him through the sunlight.

Cole crawled over to me. "I just gotta do this again."

He cupped my head with his hands and kissed me on the lips. It was as if he was telling me a complete story with that kiss.

When our lips parted, I wanted more. There was some sort of magnetism about him that made me want him more and more each time we were together.

I grabbed his head with my hands and planted another kiss on his lips. I needed to feel close to Cole, and in this moment, kissing him was the only way it would work.

After we kissed for a long while, we pulled back.

"You are amazing," Cole confessed.

"So are you," I echoed.

Cole scooted backwards as I sat up and suggested,

"Do you mind if I lie down? It's hard on my back to sit up straight."

"I'll lie down with you." Cole cleared our picnic lunch to make room on the blanket. He stuffed the wrappers into a bag and put the leftover food back into the picnic basket.

We lay down next to each other, face to face.

"That's better. Where were we before that wonderful kiss?" Cole asked.

"Visiting our parents at the cemetery," I said. We had something else in common.

I was glad Cole steered the conversation in another direction.

"Before I got a job out of state, I worked at Betty's restaurant. When I got to know Betty better, I confided in her about some things that were happening at home, and she was the one who encouraged me to move out of state. That's the reason I wanted to do everything possible to save Betty's. I've since moved back to Hill City and joined the local fire department. Our department doesn't usually come to Hill City. We're about twenty minutes outside of town." Cole adjusted his position to get a better look at me.

"Oh my goodness, we both live here? I thought you lived in New York City?"

"It's a long story, and I can't wait to tell you all about me, but tell me more about you. Did you grow up here?" Cole asked, with a soft flirty smile, as though he knew the answer.

"I grew up in Pennsylvania, but my mom moved here some years ago. I stayed with her but then, I moved to New York City. I was in a relationship that ended abruptly. It's a long story, but that's why I returned to Hill City." I didn't want to tell Cole every detail of my life just yet.

"I'm sorry to hear that. I almost forgot. I have a few homemade sugar cookies. Would you like one?"

"Sure."

Cole reached into the picnic basket and handed me a cookie.

I took a bite. "This is so good and it goes well with wine."

"Thanks. I have a sweet tooth, so I'm thankful I can bake a little," Cole laughed and took a bite of his cookie.

"So, what do you do for work?"

"I work for our local fire department." Cole winked at me.

"Oh yes, you do, don't you? Did you transfer here from the New York City Fire Department?"

"Actually, I worked in New York City, but not as a firefighter."

"So, what did you do before you moved back here?" I asked.

"I worked in hotel tourism in a big city and ended up not liking it." Cole turned over onto his back and looked into the sunlight. "I love helping people more now."

"I used to work at an advertising firm in New York City, and ended up not liking that either. I now work at St. Lucille's Nursing Home. I, too, love helping people."

"I know St. Lucille's well. My father was there for a while, and a dear friend was also there until she passed away."

"Really?"

"Yes," he said, smiling at me.

"Wow. That's where my mom was before she died."

I glanced over at Cole. His face became stoic and his eyes dreamy.

Cole turned, propped his face up on his hand, looked at me, and said, "Since we're being honest and getting to know each other, I need to tell you something. My name isn't Cole. It's Michael."

Chapter 30

Time froze. Wait! What? Cole and Michael are the same person?

"Allie, are you alright? Hello?" Cole shook my arm.

I snapped out of my daze and tried to compose myself. "Oh my . . ."

"I know this is a lot to digest, and you're likely in shock."

"Shock is an understatement," I half-whispered. *Am I ready to hear more of this story? Should I get up and leave?*

I knew I couldn't run away anymore. This tangled mess was so complicated, and those who were important to me seemed to know more than I did.

Cole looked concerned.

"So, your real name is . . . Michael?" I asked again.

"Yes, but my middle name is Cole."

"Really?" I stood up and paced trying to make sense of this revelation.

Cole watched me and said, "Yes. You can call me either Cole or Michael."

I sat back down. "Why did you mislead me when we met?" I drew in a deep breath and let it out slowly.

"I'll tell you, but first I have to tell you more about myself so you can understand why I lied."

I nodded.

"As you now know, I grew up in Hill City. I was an only child. I had a perfect family during those earlier years. Well, that is, until Mom died when I was twelve years old. From that day on, my world crumbled. Dad succumbed to alcoholism and he was rarely around. I basically raised myself. He recently died at the nursing home in town." Cole took a sip of wine.

I was intrigued by his story. How this strong man had come from a place of sadness made me appreciate him even more. My annoyance over his lying about his first name evaporated.

"School was such a blur back then. I barely graduated from high school. I had to grow up quickly because Dad wasn't capable of taking care of me. I worked part-time at Betty's to get away from the house. Working there helped my mood. After awhile, I accepted a job in Las Vegas as a representative for a major hotel chain. I was ecstatic because I could finally leave Hill City. There, I was thrown into a lifestyle of continuous entertainment, which was both new and exciting. If that wasn't fun enough, I also traveled and stayed at glamorous hotels for free. I had a place in the world. But after a while, it got to be too much." Cole took another bite of his cookie.

"Wow," I said.

"Then, Dad's nursing home called and told me about his

deteriorating health, and I knew I had to come back here. When he was dying, I met someone." Cole took another sip of wine and moved closer to me.

My heart sank. *Why is he telling me this? I don't want to hear about another woman. Oh God, is he married? And if he is, why was he with me in New York City? He was with me, wasn't he? Cole? Michael? Whoever the hell he is, he was with me. Right?*

"I'm confused. Are you married?" I braced myself for his answer.

"Huh? What gave you *that* idea?" Cole paused, searching my face.

"Well, you said you met someone."

"Oh my goodness," Cole let out a howl. "No, no, no. I didn't meet someone like *that*!" He flung his arms around me, pulled me close, and looked at me intently. "My heart is yours," he whispered, planting a kiss on me.

I wanted to pull away and think about what he was saying, but once I felt his lips on mine, all I could do was kiss him back. The man knew how to kiss, and when those lips touched mine, I melted like butter.

"I love how you kiss me," I admitted in a quiet, seductive voice.

Cole moaned, "Do we have to stop?"

"Yes, I want to hear more of your story," I said, slowly pulling myself away from him. We could've kissed until sunset.

"Okay. But for the record, I do love kissing you," he said smiling. "So, where were we? Oh yes, the other woman."

"So, if she wasn't a love interest, who was she?"

"Her name was Lina, short for Carolina," Cole said. "Your mother."

Chapter 31

*J*ust last week, we stood outside Café Amor and Cole said he knew Mom.

"My mom? So, you really did know her?"

Cole looked at me. "Yes," he said slowly. "I knew your mom."

It was quiet all of a sudden. I've waited so long to find someone who knew her and I was dumbfounded that it was Cole, a man I had met at a bar in New York City.

"But how? When?"

"I'd love to tell you," he said.

I cleared my throat. "Before you start, I have to confess something. Since you know a lot about me already, I should tell you my real name isn't Allie."

"Yes, I know. Your name's Faith." He looked deep into my eyes. "I'm sorry if this is awkward."

"How do you know my . . ."

"I'll tell you how I learned your first name in a bit," Cole said with a chuckle.

How much more does he know about me? I felt mixed emotions that ranged from being elated that Cole may have the answers I was searching for to being annoyed that he hadn't told me any of this sooner.

"I can appreciate how you must be feeling," Cole said. He looked contemplative and shifted his body on the blanket.

When I nodded, he reached for my hand. "If I give you too much information or you want me to stop, let me know. Your mom hoped you would circle back to Hill City. She really wanted us to meet."

I smiled and marveled at how all this time Mom was playing matchmaker!

"I met your mom at St. Lucille's when I visited my dad who was dying." Cole looked at me.

"What a small world." I couldn't believe what I was hearing.

Cole nodded. "Your mom was an inspiration to me because of the way she cared for my dad. They were good friends. We often talked about him, and, eventually, she opened up about you. I was intrigued and wanted to know all about you. She shared her one photo of you and I thought you were, are, so beautiful. I was drawn to you by how she described you."

"Wow." I liked hearing what Mom said about me. "I suppose you wonder why I wasn't there with her. Like you, I have my own story."

"Well, I did wonder why the two of you hadn't stayed in contact. I'd love to hear your story. Maybe during our next date?" Cole winked at me.

"Okay, go on." *This is his time.*

"She loved you so much, and this may sound crazy, but

as she talked about you, I found myself longing to meet you. I was developing all these ideas about you—what you looked like and what you'd be like. I think I'm a pretty good judge of character. Did you know that your mom's nickname for you was Bree? After she passed, I learned that Brielle is your middle name and Faith is your first name."

"Yes, that's right."

"Are you still feeling okay?" Cole asked.

"Yes, I'm sorry I didn't tell you my real name sooner."

"I understand. You didn't know who I was or when you'd see me again. And I wasn't being honest with you about my first name either. When I found out that your name was Faith, I knew we were meant for each other. Before I met your mom, I didn't have much faith. I didn't like who I was and I was plagued by bad luck. Talking with your mom, learning more about Dad, and about you, faith had a way of creeping back into my life. How could I not fall for a mysterious woman named Faith?"

My face felt warm. Cole poured us more wine. We clanked our glasses and took a sip.

"Your mom said you love puzzles, and learning about you has been like a puzzle of sorts. I bet your life is somewhat of a puzzle, too, right?" He looked at me.

"Oh yes, you don't know the half of it," I chimed.

"I may know more than you think . . ." Cole hinted.

"Really? Oh, my goodness, this gets more interesting by the minute."

"Your mom was such a gift when my father was dying. I didn't know much about him and I had very little respect for him, until your mom told me what kind of man he was. I can't wait to explain how I came into your life."

Cole inched closer and draped his arm around my waist. He reached over and kissed me.

After the kiss, Cole continued with his story. "So, I bonded with my dad and your mom. A few weeks later, Dad passed away while I was by his side," he paused.

"Oh no, I'm so sorry to hear that," I said, pulling him close in a hug.

"The first hug after Dad passed was from your mom, and the second hug is from you right now. Our parents must be smiling from heaven." He hugged me tight.

I nestled my face into his chest. It felt so good to be with him. Eventually, we pulled away from each other.

"After he passed, your mom and I came here for a picnic, at this exact spot, to celebrate Dad's life and our love for him." Cole waved his arms around the area.

"Really? You two were *here?*" *If only I'd kept in touch with Mom, I would've met Cole a lot sooner.*

"It's bittersweet, isn't it?" Cole shifted back a couple inches so he could see my face. "Following the picnic, Lina and I went to Dad's house. He had given me a key that opened a secret box that was hidden in the floor in my bedroom. You and I both like mysteries."

My eyes widened. "What was in the box?"

"There were special keepsakes my parents had kept since I was a baby: my birth certificate, a lock of my hair, and some loving messages my parents wrote to each other after I was born. I was so touched that they had kept these things and that Dad saved them for me. He was very ill most of his life. I still don't know how he put these things together and came up with the idea of hiding them in the floor in my bedroom. Also, there was a letter that he and my mom wrote to me when she was alive, probably just before she passed away. I never knew until I found the box that such a letter existed. It was beautiful." Cole wiped his eyes.

"Oh, that's so sweet and sad. What did the letter say?"

"I can read it to you sometime, but basically it said how I'd changed their lives and how happy I made them. They wrote about how we loved each other, and shared happy memories. The letter was written by Dad and signed by Mom. She was so weak from the cancer. Her writing was frail and lopsided. If I had something like this right after she had passed, maybe I would've felt less anger and abandonment when Dad succumbed to drinking. Better late than never, I guess, but it really made me weep." Cole moved closer to me. "Can I get another hug?"

"Of course you can. Thank you for sharing this with me." I hugged him tight. "So, then what happened?"

"Two weeks after I arrived back in Las Vegas, I got a call from St. Lucille's that your mom had passed." Cole stopped talking, looked at me, and gently stroked my arm.

"I feel horrible that I wasn't with her," I said. Sadness set in and I felt as though we had rewound time as we went through this loss together. My heart fell. Cole was one of the last people to spend time with Mom.

"I hate to interrupt, but did you meet someone named Gracie?"

"I can't say I remember her. Who's that?"

"She was Mom's good friend who was with her before she passed. She also taught me more about my mom."

"What do you mean, Gracie taught you more about your mom?" Cole cocked his head.

"I'll tell you later. I'm quite sure that my mom appreciated your friendship. Thank you for spending time with her when you were in town. It breaks my heart that I was too late to see her." I looked away, briefly collecting my thoughts.

"I'm sure your mother would understand. So, a month after Dad died, I received a package in the mail that changed my life."

Chapter 32

"I thought I changed your life," I teased.

"Yes, you did, but not until after I received that package."

"I'm dying to know. What was inside?"

"Before I tell you, I think we should go back to your place. It's getting dark, and I'm sure we'll be hungry soon. Let's walk and talk." Cole stood up.

"Sounds good to me. This is the perfect time for a break, even though I still have a ton of questions."

We folded the blanket and grabbed the picnic basket. Before we left, I tugged at Cole's arm and said, "Come with me for a sec."

We walked over to the edge of the canyon and looked across the horizon. I turned to face Cole. "I still can't believe we met in New York City, and now we're here, at the exact same place we've been before with other people. It's like we've come full circle." My eyes misted. "I really like you, Cole."

I stood on my tippy toes, draped my arms around

his neck and pulled him to me. Looking into his eyes, I stole a kiss. His mouth felt more familiar than before.

"I'm so glad you're here with me," I whispered.

"Me too. Our paths led us to each other."

Before we left, Cole called to order a pizza. Then we held hands as we walked back to my place, admiring the scenery. The sky darkened and the moon shone, round and majestic. We marveled at how much more we could see compared to the skyline in New York City. The stars sparkled.

The pizza delivery car arrived when we got to the cottage. Cole paid the driver and carried the pizza into the house.

"I can't remember the last time I've had pizza," I said. My nostrils breathed in the doughy pepperoni smell. I was starving.

"I love pizza," Cole mused.

I went to the kitchen and found two paper plates and a bottle of red wine. I walked to the couch and sat down, handing Cole a plate.

"We're going to be all wined out," Cole laughed.

"Here's to revealing mysteries, secrets, and puzzles," I toasted as we took a sip of wine.

As we faced each other on the couch, I said, "I'm so hungry . . . I've waited long enough. Tell me more of your story."

"Oh, alright," Cole winked at me, as he ate his slice of pizza.

"I'm dying to hear who the package was from and what was inside," I said between bites.

"Oh, yes. The package was from my dad and your mom." Cole looked at me.

"Huh? From my mom? I'm confused."

"Yes, from your mom and my dad," Cole repeated.

"Tell me more." The words flew out of my mouth.

"Inside the package were the ashes of both our parents."

"Wait. I thought Mom was buried?"

"Yes, she is, well, half of her ashes are buried."

"What do you mean half of her ashes? Is that even possible?"

"I was just as surprised as you are. In a letter from my dad, he said his ashes were buried next to my mom, but he wanted me to have the other half. He alluded to your mom wanting this for you, too."

"I've never heard of such a thing. How strange." I ripped off some pizza crust and took a bite.

"It's new to me too."

"Go on, I can't wait to hear more." I drank some wine.

"In his letter, my dad said he loved me and he was with Mom where he belonged. It's almost like he mailed it from heaven. He said they would watch over me. But that was the gist of it. Also, in the package was a check. I'm not sure how he saved up so much money because our house looked like it belonged to someone who was dead poor. But I took the check to the bank and it cashed. I was burnt out at work, so I quit my job. The only thing I really wanted to do was to find you. Not only did I have your mom's ashes to deliver, but I also wanted to meet you. I had this feeling about us, and something was telling me I needed to explore it."

"What was . . ."

"Hang on, I'm not done, sweetie." Cole smiled at me. "Attached to your mom's ashes was a note with Terese's name and phone number. The note said that Terese was your best friend, and she would know how to find you."

My eyes widened. *I knew it! She was in on this!*

"The agreement I had with Terese was that she wouldn't tell me about you, but instead where I could find you. I desperately wanted to meet you, and if we met and hit it off, I wanted to hear your story directly from you."

As he talked, Terese's actions resurfaced. Looking back, it made perfect sense.

"The first time I saw you was at The Vintage. I was sitting in the cor—"

"Yes! I remember that! Oh my God, that was you? But you looked different."

"Yep, that was me. I had a hat on. I was too nervous to approach you and I didn't know what you knew. I wasn't sure if Terese told you about me."

"I can't believe that was you! Did you know I felt something when I looked at you then?"

"Had I known we were feeling the same thing, I would've definitely had enough confidence to approach you. While you had no idea who I was, I knew about you," Cole mused.

He set down his plate and moved on top of me. His body pressed into mine, and if that wasn't heavenly enough, he planted kisses on my lips and neck. Returning his kisses, my body pressed into his, feeling those same sensations run marathons up and down my spine, traveling back in time, to that moment at The Vintage. We groaned in unison.

Afterwards, I got up and led Cole into the bedroom. I wanted to lie down next to him, and hear more of his incredible story, which was beginning to sound like a fairy tale.

Pulling the blankets over us, he said, "The time after that was at the drug store here in Hill City. You were coming out just as I was going in and—"

"Oh my goodness! I thought you looked familiar. I was so embarrassed. I didn't know what to say." *How many other places had he seen me?*

As if he were reading my mind, Cole nodded. "Little did you know the first time you returned to New York City, I paid for your ticket. It was Valentine's weekend."

"You did? You didn't even know me, and I didn't know how lucky I was. Thank you so much." Memories from that special night with Cole rushed to the forefront of my mind. I remembered how intoxicating his cologne smelled that evening.

"You're welcome. Luckily, I had the courage to approach you and ask for a dance. I had black hair at the time, not this blonde messy mop." He ruffled his hand through his hair and chuckled.

"That's when I lied about my name," Allie said.

Cole grinned and continued. "That first night we were together was magical. I never felt that kind of passion with a woman before. I felt like a virgin in many ways because it was so new, and so connecting." Cole's foot touched mine.

"Me, too. I've never made love like that before, and it was so out of character for me. I was reeling from a loss, but under normal circumstances, I never would've done something like that. I really didn't think we would meet again, but deep down, I hoped we would," I admitted.

Cole smiled and nodded. "So, after our beautiful night, I really didn't know when I'd see you again. Terese told me you were busy in Hill City living your own life. I was at a standstill for a while and felt sorry for myself. I wondered if you'd ever return to New York City to stay. My job had transferred me there. All I needed was for you to come back, and then we would've met a lot sooner."

I reached for his hand. "But, remember, we saw each other at that Japanese restaurant later in the spring. That was so weird seeing you there of all places."

"Oh, yes! You're right. We were naughty, weren't we? I loved kissing you, while our friends were inside waiting for us," Cole laughed. "Actually, Terese texted me and said you'd be there with her. I told a little fib that day."

"Oh, *really*? What was the fib?"

"That I was there with a friend. Actually, when you returned to your table, Terese was outside talking with *me*," Cole shared.

"Wow, you were the friend she was talking to? I had no idea. The time we spent together was always at the forefront of my mind. Since I met you, I had fleeting thoughts of what it would be like to allow love back into my life."

"I'm happy to hear that. There was something about you that intrigued me. Then, one night I received a call from Terese. Whenever she called, I worried she would say that she had revealed everything to you. Luckily, she just said you were returning to New York City to celebrate your one-year anniversary of your move. This is when we hooked up at Gaby's again and made love. It was so hard to leave you afterwards, but I knew I had to. I was already becoming attached to you. I didn't know if that would be the last time, I'd ever see you, and I didn't want to scare you away so I took what I could. I know that was selfish of me."

Pieces of my life were slowly coming together to create

the answers I'd been searching for. I felt lucky to be with Cole.

The wine and pizza made me feel sleepy, but I wanted to hear more of his story. I willed my eyes to remain open.

"The next time after that was at Café Amor. We met there, I'm quite sure you remember," Cole said.

"A part of me was disappointed when Michael didn't show. So, when you showed up, it was awkward. I wasn't expecting to see you, but I was glad we met up again, until you told me about Mom and then I got upset and ran away. I'm good at running," I said.

"Another similarity. So am I. The next time I ran into you was at the cemetery when I had Hal with me. On a side note, this is something you may find pretty cool. One day, after I moved back to Hill City, I found Hal at the same place where we had our picnic. He must've been lost, and no one ever claimed him. I named him after my dad."

"Very cool. He's such a cute puppy. And smart, too," I paused. "So, how did you decide to stay here indefinitely?"

"When I got the money from my dad, that solidified the decision to stay here. My original plan before getting the check was to move here and travel for my job. But I wasn't exactly sure how that would work since I didn't have enough money in my savings. With Dad's check, I was able to quit my job and take a leap of faith. Just so you know, I live slightly outside the city limits of Hill City. After I moved here, I found a job with our local fire department."

"It's amazing how similar our stories are. Without going into much detail, the same thing happened to me. After staying here for a while, I wanted to move here permanently. I was glad that St. Lucille's hired me."

"I wonder how we missed each other since we were both at St. Lucille's," Cole contemplated.

"Oh, I started working there after my mom passed away. I believe in timing in life. Even if we had bumped into each other there earlier, our timing may've been off. I'm so thankful we are together now," I confessed.

"Me, too. That was quite the detour in my story. So, backing up, when we were standing in the rain outside your house, after I followed you home from the cemetery, I told you I loved you. Remember?"

"Crystal clear. I didn't understand what I now know about you. I thought, who is this crazy guy saying he loves me without knowing me?" I remembered how angry I felt standing in the rain getting soaking wet.

"That was the third time we made love. You were so hot; I couldn't keep my hands off you. I've been falling in love with you ever since Lina told me about you."

"I felt like I was in a romance novel. There we were, making love during a thunderstorm before we really knew each other. Then, when I woke up the next day, you were gone. I still have the note you left. I've kept all your notes, as though they were the last thread of hope that you may return. In that note, you alluded to having Faith. This is when I wondered whether you knew my first name."

"Ha. I did that on purpose. Your full name was written on your mom's ashes. Every time we were together, for me, it was a minute closer to when I could divulge everything I'm telling you now. I couldn't wait for that to happen." Cole squeezed my hand. "So, then, our next meeting was at Betty's during the fire. Thank you so much for being with me in the ambulance and at the hospital. That meant a lot to me."

"No place I would've rather been," I whispered.

Cole gasped. "Oh shit, I forgot to tell you the most important thing about the package. There was a sealed envelope addressed to you from your mom."

Cole dug into his pocket, pulled it out, and handed it to me.

Chapter 33

I carefully opened the letter and handed it back to Cole. "Please, read it to me."

June 17, 2012

Faith Brielle Neely:

I love and miss you so much. The fact that you're reading this may mean someone found you and told you a few things about what happened to me. It may also mean that you've returned to Hill City. I can only hope, and here's why.

My story dates back to many years ago, when I was in Hill City for work and met your father. His name was Michael—

"Oh my goodness. My dad's name was Michael? How could I've forgotten that?"

"Wow, I have your father's name. No wonder she liked my name," Cole said.

It was love at first sight. We had one night of fiery passion, and when I went back to Philly, I learned I was pregnant with you. My whole life changed. After you were born, I moved back to Hill City to be with your father. We were so in love, but it was really hard to make ends meet. I had no job, and his job was sporadic.

Michael ended up leaving us when you were three years old, which broke my heart. I was a total wreck and didn't know how I'd ever manage taking care of you by myself, but you saved me. We moved back to Philly, and before you left for New York City, we moved back to Hill City. This was home for us. It's where our life together started, and where I felt the most comfortable.

I knew you wanted to venture out on your own, that you were getting tired living with your mama, but I didn't like that you were with this Daniel fellow, someone you barely knew. At the same time, I understood because I went through something similar with your father.

You and I were in contact a lot at first, but our communication started to dwindle, and then I didn't hear from you anymore. Many times, I called you, and either no one answered or the operator said the phone was disconnected.

I wasn't sure what happened to you, and my heart broke again.

"Wow, I didn't know she tried to call me," I said.

Faith Bree, you need to know that I've never blamed you. You and I were always close, and my instincts suggested that our disconnect was because of Daniel. My health was declining, and I wasn't able to track you down. But I found Terese's phone number so I reached out to her. I was losing my memory and was afraid if you called, I might not remember you. I begged her not to tell you about me.

I didn't want to hurt you by not remembering you. Around that time, I moved into Beacon Light Nursing Home and later met a nice young man named Michael.

Cole stopped reading and winked at me.

Puzzled, I asked, "Where's Beacon Light Nursing Home?"

"Apparently, St. Lucille's used to be called Beacon Light. Lucille means light. They changed the name right after Dad died."

I nodded for him to continue reading.

Michael was visiting his father, Hal, who was my good friend. I really like Michael. Not only do I love his name because it reminds me of your father, but he's handsome and like you in so many ways. There's also my good friend, Gracie, whom you may or may not know. Gracie is married to Lance. Hal is Lance's best friend and we all met at a barn dance many years ago.

"I knew Lance, but I didn't know that your dad was Lance's best friend," I said.

"This is news to me," Cole chimed.

Anyway, my bases were covered—there were several people who could, hopefully, lead you back to Hill City to learn what happened to me and possibly lead you to real love, because you deserve to be happy, baby. I'm hoping Michael is my messenger and that he's delivering this letter to you right now.

Cole paused and looked at me. "Wow, according to your mom, our parents were at the same barn dance. My parents met there, and it seems like Gracie met her husband there too. I bet if we were closer to our parents, we would've met a lot sooner," he winked and sipped some water. "How are you doing?"

"Good," I said. I couldn't believe what I was hearing. I was thankful it was dark in my bedroom because tears were collecting on my pillow. Learning about Mom and Cole was a bigger piece of something, and I was smack in the middle. This was all unraveling right in front of me.

I hope Terese was able to secure the cottage for you. Your dad left me the cottage when he left us. It's where your father and I conceived you and where we lived for three years as a family.

"Wow! No wonder this place feels familiar. I'm so glad I live here now. I feel her presence sometimes," I said.

I asked Gracie to take care of the cottage for me. Selling it was never an option because it meant so much to us. I wanted to tell you the story when you were with me, but I couldn't find the words. I was still reeling from a mix of anger and sadness about your father leaving us behind.

Hearing this, I felt closer to Mom. Dad left her, just like Daniel left me.

Cole put down the letter, and edged towards me. His hands gently grabbed my body and pulled me to him. "This is amazing. I'm learning, too."

I hugged him back and nestled my head into his chest. I was glad he was here with me.

Cole's hand made its way to my chin and tipped it up. I closed my eyes and our lips met in a beautiful kiss. This time it had more meaning, and more momentum, knowing what we now know about this place.

We were only half-way through the letter. I loved

learning about Mom. Even though Cole and I had made love, we had never connected emotionally until tonight.

My mind drifted back to the letter from Mom. Tears streamed down my face.

Sitting up, I threw off the blankets and ran outside. Holding onto the railing, I walked down the back porch stairs, and stopped mid-step.

"What's wrong?" Cole huffed behind me.

Electricity penetrated my body, harder than at the cemetery or when I saw the deer or the butterfly.

Cole's arms wrapped around me from behind, and I turned to face him, overcome with emotion, unable to speak.

"I know," he said. "This is very real for you. You feel her, don't you?"

Between sobs, I began, "This is so hard for me. I never meant to hurt her. A few people said things like it was nice to see me, and one man even sounded *mad* at me for coming back. I never knew what they meant, but now everything makes sense. This was out of my control. I wasn't aware Mom was dying. I never intended to let her die alone."

"You didn't know your mom was dying?" Cole looked at me, and hugged me. "Shh," he said, trying to comfort me. "It's okay. You can trust me."

"Something happened to me when I was with my ex-boyfriend, which wiped out most of my memory. A couple months ago, Gracie and Terese filled in pieces of my life. Then I met you, and you gave me more information about my mom including this wonderful letter."

I paused, wiping the tears off my face. "I don't know how to prove to you that I'm a good person."

"Shh, you know what? I believe you. That's all there's to it. Your story is just as important as mine, and as your mom's. I believe you."

As soon as Cole said those three words to me, a weight lifted. *He believes me!*

I couldn't hold back any longer. Hugging him, I whispered, "Cole, I'm falling in love with you."

"I'm falling in love with you, too."

At that moment, I knew Cole was the one for me. I didn't want anyone else, but at the same time, letting someone in again was scary. I was afraid of being hurt and going through the spiral I'd gone through with Daniel, but I knew I needed to take the risk. This was the closest I'd ever come to being in true love. My love story was beginning, finally.

After he gently kissed my forehead and combed his fingers through my hair, Cole led me back into the warm house, to my bedroom and into bed.

Cole held me and whispered in my ear, "Faith, I can't tell you how much I want to make love to you right now. I've never felt this close to anyone."

Hearing him say my first name for the first time and in the same sentence as making love, was incredible.

"But I want to finish honoring your mom by continuing to read her letter to you."

"Yes, I want you to continue. Thank you for reading it to me. I'll never forget this night with you."

I hope that with their combined effort, Terese and Michael were able to get you back to Hill City, full circle to where you and I were last together. I will always love you. I've learned a lot about myself over the last few years of my life, and I don't regret anything that's happened because I was able to fall in love with your father, and be your mother, two of my greatest joys in life even though both were short lived.

By the time you get this letter, I've likely passed on. I've lived a long life, and I am truly thankful. Look for me in nature, animals, or the sunset in Hill City from my favorite lookout spot. Gracie, my dear friend, knows where it is and can show you. She frequents the nursing home in town.

I want you to know that I've always loved you and will continue to love you from heaven. I know you'll feel me. Have Faith.

This brings me to your name. When I first stepped into Hill City, before you were born, I believed in faith and that everything would work out the way it was supposed to. I believed in Michael and our love, and we believed in you. When things were really hard, I still had faith. That's where the idea came for your name. I wanted you to have faith and to be named Faith.

Faith, my wish for you is to find true love and peace. I'm always with you, and I love you with all my heart. - Mama

Chapter 34

I rolled over and opened my eyes. Cole was sleeping quietly next to me. He hadn't left; in fact, this was the first time he wasn't gone when I woke up. I smiled and snuggled into his shoulder, draping my arm across his broad chest. *I can't wait to read Mama's letter again.*

I watched Cole's chest move up and down as he breathed, grateful for him and for our long journey together. All that happens, like Mom said, will work out.

Cole woke up and kissed my cheeks. "Good morning, beautiful," he whispered.

My heart skipped a beat. "Good morning, handsome." I hugged his body.

The last time I woke up in bed with a man was with Daniel. My hand flew to my head and combed through my hair.

"You look beautiful, don't change a thing." Cole kissed my head.

I smiled.

"We must've fallen asleep," he said.

"When you stopped reading, I cuddled up next to you and I was out." *I love being close to this man!*

"Holding you in my arms reminds me of all the other times we held each other after we made love. You make me so happy." Cole tightened his grip.

"Thanks for sticking around this morning and not rushing out the door."

Cole kissed my eyelids. "Reading that letter from your mom last night, living with you through your emotions, and experiencing some of them myself made me realize how much more I'm falling for you. The last thing I'd ever want to do is leave."

I looked up at him, and his lips covered mine in a deep kiss, which turned fiery fast. Immediately, Cole was on top of me, and we were grinding our bodies together in hot passion.

His hands cupped my head and a bolt of electricity raced up my spine. Cole's eyes looked deeply into mine, and our lips pressed together in another kiss. His tongue explored my mouth, as his hardness pulsated on my inner thigh. Fire blazed inside my chest, ready to explode any minute. Cole moved up and down over me, grazing my nipples and turning them hard. His stiff masculinity probed for an opening. My legs were wet and the aching inside me was screaming desire. My body arched, and his manhood finally slid inside. My hands grasped his muscular back and pulled him deeper into me. The heat that burned inside raged. Our rhythm strengthened and beat faster, and faster and . . .

With one final push, we both swelled. Cole yelled in

a triumphant groan of delight, and I joined him a second later. The feeling of pleasure continued to spin, turn and pulsate repeatedly.

Our rhythm and breathing subsided. Cole rolled over next to me and let out a sigh. "Oh my God, Faith, you rock my world!"

"I feel so close to you."

After a while, Cole kissed my face. "I'm starving."

"So am I." As I lay there, I wondered whether I was conceived in this very room.

"Darling, why don't you freshen up and I'll go make you something good to eat. Did I mention I love to cook?" Cole got out of bed and put on my robe that was hanging in the closet.

"You're too good to be true. Am I dreaming?"

"We aren't dreaming, but it feels so good, doesn't it? Every day, I thank God I found you." Cole winked, and motioned for me to go into the bathroom.

After brushing my teeth, I walked into the kitchen. Cole was sitting on the back porch. A delicious aroma filled the air.

"Hey, what's for breakfast?" I teased.

"There you are. You're gorgeous in the sunlight." Cole stood up. "I've made eggs with bacon and hot tea. Go make yourself at home on the porch and I'll serve you." Cole walked past me and dished out breakfast.

I went onto the porch and sat down. There was a red rose in a vase on the table. Knowing this porch belonged to my parents gave it new meaning.

It was warm and sunny, and there was so much peace today, inside my heart and mind, as well as outside the cottage.

Cole came out and handed me a plate with two eggs, bacon, an apple, and hot tea. He went back inside to fetch his plate.

"Where did the rose come from?" I asked, smiling up at him.

"Happy Valentine's Day. When I realized it was today, I worked my magic for my one and only valentine."

"That's so thoughtful. Thank you. You're my valentine, too." Being with Cole was indeed magical, and holidays now had new meaning.

"It's a miracle that we're together," Cole beamed.

I smiled and took a bite of the eggs, which melted in my mouth. "This is the best breakfast I've ever had. It's so flavorful. Thank you for making it."

"You're most welcome. I look forward to making breakfast for you every day."

I looked up at the sky. *Thank you, Mom, for sending Cole to me. I miss you so much. I hope you're here with us.*

Cole and I talked about our favorite foods, the music we like, and adventures on our bucket lists, like traveling to Hawaii and Australia.

One important topic was the letters.

"So, tell me about the letters at Mom's grave. Did you put them there? Was the one you gave me in New York City a part of that sequence?" I took a bite of my apple.

"Yes and yes." Cole sipped his tea.

"Were the letters written by your dad for my mom? Now that I know about their friendship, did he have a thing for her?"

"Keep guessing," Cole winked at me.

"I've run through all the scenarios in my head. First, I thought they were from a man who was pining for my mom. Now that I know you put them there, I'm not sure the reason."

"Faith, I wrote those letters, like the one I left for you in New York City."

"I'm confused," I said.

"You have to understand something. When your mom told me all about you, I started to develop feelings for you. Then when we met at various places, I fell for you, slowly at first. When we kept making love, my feelings grew. But I didn't know how to get you to notice me once you moved here. I tried putting flowers at your mom's gravesite hoping it would pique your interest. One day, I saw you at the cemetery, so I had the idea to put the letters there." Cole took a bite of his apple, his eyes never leaving mine.

"Ok, go on," I said, trying to understand.

"So, I left those letters at the gravesite. They confessed my feelings for you. The letters were never intended for your mom; they were intended for you."

My fork fell out of my hand and onto the ground.

"Oops," I said, bending down to retrieve it. I placed it back on the table and walked over to Cole.

He stood up.

I draped my arms around his broad chest and pulled him to me.

"Where did you come from? Are you for real? Thank you for the letters with your confessions. I can't believe they were for me. You were sneaky to leave numbers on the letters so I wouldn't stop looking for them. I never imagined they would be for anyone but Mom. I don't know what else to say."

"Seeing your cute reaction is all I need; you don't need to say anything else," Cole mused.

"So, how did you get the letter to Gayle at St. Lucille's? She said you dropped it off after Mom passed."

"Actually, I went in there earlier the same week that you received it. I had to convince Gayle who I was, that I was legit and to give you my letter. She was very protective of you. Finally, she gave in. She said if anyone deserved to find love, it was you."

"She is so sweet." *I knew it! Gayle was also in on this scheme.*

"Your mom told me you liked puzzles, so this was meant to be a puzzle of sorts. It's surprising you thought the letters were for your mom. I hadn't thought about that twist. Now you know they were for you, and only you."

Chapter 35

Cole and I went back to work the next week. We often talked on the phone at night. The more we were apart, the more I missed him.

I arranged for my two closest friends to meet me at Betty's on Monday, so I could share the most recent happenings in my life.

The owners had repaired the fire damage, so Betty's was open for business again. The door chimed as I walked inside.

Gayle and Gracie were sitting at a booth. They both turned to look at me.

I ran to their booth and gave each of them a big hug.

"Hi. I'm so happy to see both of you," I gushed.

"Hi, Faith," they said, together.

"Do sit down. We want to hear all about what you've been up to," Gayle said.

The waitress came over to take our order and I began my story.

"If either of you know more about what's going on than

I do, feel free to chime in." I looked at them and took a sip of water. "It turns out my Mom orchestrated a number of surprises for me."

Gracie raised her eyebrows.

"The last time we talked, there was a mysterious man named Michael, who had left a letter with Gayle after Mom died. Anyway, after I moved here, I often visited New York City to see my best friend, Terese. When we went out on the town, I usually ran into a handsome man named Cole and we had some steamy experiences together," I giggled.

The waitress walked over with our food. I nibbled on my salad. I was excited to tell my friends this news.

"Ooh la la," Gayle chimed in. "Do go on."

"To make a long story short, Cole's first name is Michael."

"Yeah, and?" Gracie asked.

"And, as it turns out, Michael is Cole. He's one person. Cole is his middle name."

"Oh my. So, the man behind the letters was Cole?" Gayle had already put the pieces together.

"You got it!" I could hardly contain my excitement.

"So, I did meet him when he came in recently to give me that letter for you," Gayle winked at me.

"Yes, you did. I had no idea he gave you that letter that same week you gave it to me. I'm going to refer to Michael as Cole, because that's what I call him. So, when Mom was at St. Lucille's, she met Cole, who was there to visit his dad, Hal. Gracie, I think, you know Hal too, right?" I looked at her.

"Yes, you're right. My Lance was Hal's best friend. You've done your research," Gracie smiled.

"As Mom talked about me, Cole started to fall in love

with me. So, after Cole's father died, he received a package with a check, along with half of Mom's ashes."

"What? Isn't your mom buried in the cemetery?" Gracie asked.

"Yes, she is. But only half her ashes are buried there. She had requested that the other half be given to me."

"Oh, my. I don't get why she did that, but okay, go on. This is a very interesting twist," Gracie said.

"Eventually, Cole ended up moving back to Hill City, his hometown, using his father's money. He became a firefighter here. So, that night when I was expecting to meet Michael at Café Amor, I saw Cole instead, which was no coincidence." I glanced at Gayle and then Gracie.

"It's okay, Gracie knows," Gayle said, as if she were reading my mind.

"Good. That night at Café Amor, Cole told me he knew Mom. I got upset and left the café in a huff. The next day, Cole saw me at the cemetery and later told me he loved me." I glanced at my two friends who motioned for me to go on.

"I got upset again, not understanding how Cole could fall in love with me so quickly. Well, one thing led to another, and we ended up in bed." I didn't care that I was sharing these details. Both women knew me well, and giggled.

"Then, Cole gave me a letter from Mom. It was in the package from his father."

"What did it say?" Gracie wondered.

"She shared more of her story, including some things I forgot about. She also told me how she met Michael, who is really Cole."

"So, what's next? Do you have another date planned?" Gayle asked.

"Not yet. I wanna tell Cole more about me. I'm thinking about taking him to New York City to tell him there. This is where our story started."

"That's a wonderful idea. Let us know what happens. I think I speak for both of us when I say we are so happy you found Cole, and your way back to your mom. We wish you both all the best. You seem to really like him."

∽ ∾

Later that week, I called Cole to talk about visiting New York City. He thought it was a great idea. It was Wednesday, and I booked a flight for Friday for a long weekend.

I called Terese and when her answering machine came on, I said, "Hi, Terese. This is Faith. I'm coming to New York City this Friday for a visit and I'm bringing someone that I want you to meet. Please call me."

Friday came quickly. By the time Cole and I were boarding the plane, I still hadn't heard back from Terese. It was surreal going on our first plane trip together. He let me have the window seat after we stuffed our bags into the overhead compartments.

As I sat down in the narrow seat, my phone beeped. I missed a call from Terese. She left a message explaining that she was out of town for work, but we could stay at her place. I told Cole that she would text me the code to get into her building, the key was under her door mat, and that she would be home in a couple days.

"That's so nice of her," Cole said. "Is that what we'll do then?"

"Sure, we can stay at her place. I have her address in my phone. It sounds like she'll be home the day before we fly back to Hill City. It's so cool that we're making this trip together," I said, beaming from ear to ear.

"I know, honey. I can't wait to hear more of your story." Cole leaned back and closed his eyes.

The plane rolled down the runway and rose into the air. My ears popped. I held Cole's hand as the takeoff rocked us to sleep. When the flight attendant came by for drinks, I peeked at Cole who was still sleeping. Leaning against his muscular shoulder, I closed my eyes and fell back asleep.

It was early in the afternoon when the pilot's voice woke us up. Once the plane landed, it took us a while to filter outside through the crowd. It was freezing. We quickly flagged down a cab.

"I still can't believe we're here together. This trip has a lot of firsts for us—first time making love, first flight, first time staying together at Terese's place, first time being together for an entire getaway," I said.

"I know, beautiful. I'm so blessed to be here with you. There's nowhere else I'd rather be."

The cab pulled up to Terese's place and Cole paid the driver. The code worked for the door of her building and the key was, indeed, under her door mat. I unlocked the door and we walked in. The place was just as I had remembered. I led Cole into the guest bedroom where we unpacked our bags and crashed onto the bed.

"Our trip went fast! I guess that's because we were sleeping most of the time," Cole said, closing his eyes.

"Yep." I propped my head on my hand and looked at him. He was handsome in his tan pants and plaid, long-sleeved, button-down shirt. I started to unbutton his shirt.

"Hmmm," Cole said softly.

My lips found his naked chest and I began giving him

small kisses. Cole's breathing slowed. When I looked at him, he was sound asleep. I closed my eyes and drifted into a deep sleep in the crook of his arm.

When Cole woke up, he kissed my face. I opened my eyes and the bedroom was dark.

"What time is it?" I asked, rubbing my eyes.

"It's late. I think we're sleep deprived," Cole chuckled.

"Lying next to you is so relaxing. But really, what time is it?"

"It's 7:00 p.m. and I'm starving," Cole said.

"Let's go get something to eat. How about Gaby's for old time's sake?"

"That's a great idea," Cole said.

We bundled up and went outside to hail a cab. When we got there, we walked in. Memories of my first visit came flooding back.

"Wow, we're actually back where we first met," I chimed, feeling giddy.

I grabbed the high-top table where Terese and I first sat and we looked at the menu. We both ordered a burger and fries. I ordered a mudslide, and Cole ordered a draft beer.

"I'm reminiscing about the last time we were here. Remember, when we met near the bathroom? You didn't think you knew me and . . ."

"After you kissed me, it all came rushing back," I said, finishing his sentence. I took a sip of my drink. "Wow, this is strong."

Cole smiled at me. "Good."

"Why good?"

"I have a surprise for you," he winked at me.

Puzzled, I looked at him. Then, our food arrived.

I didn't want to tell Cole my story tonight. I needed time to think about what I would say. As if on cue, the music started to blare in the background.

"The music is so loud. I'll tell you my story tomorrow, I promise." I reached across the table and held his hand.

We finished our meal and Cole paid for our food. Then, he pulled me onto the dance floor and swung me around. We danced slowly and held each other close, even though the rhythm was fast. I smelled beer on his breath and was sure he could smell the Bailey's on mine.

Cole's hand cupped my head, a gesture I loved, and his lips found mine.

A slow song played, and our feet slowed down even more. Cole pulled me closer. His eyes found mine, and he looked into them, as though he was looking into my soul. I hugged his body and smiled.

Before the song was over, Cole led me off the dance floor.

"Where are we going?" I yelled.

Cole didn't say anything as we grabbed our jackets, and went outside.

"I could barely hear you. That music was so loud," he said.

"Where are we going?" I asked again.

"Somewhere special," Cole said, putting his arm around me and walking in step with me.

I smiled.

We walked to the rooftop where we had been the first night we met. Bright stars filled the dark sky and colorful lights shone down below. The gazebo was still here.

Cole led me inside and said, "Kiss me. I love kissing you."

I stood near the window, draped my arms around his

neck, and slowly kissed him. He pinned me against the wall and fiercely kissed me back, his tongue chasing mine.

Cole led me to the chaise lounge where we first made love. He took off my coat. Then, he unzipped my jeans and unbuttoned my shirt. Cole quickly pulled his coat off, unzipped his pants, unbuttoned his shirt, and laid me down gently. The light from the moon outlined his body. He lay on top of me and began pulsating with rapid energy. We moved to our own rhythm and melted together. Cole was in full force. He murmured that he wanted to be with me forever, that he'd never leave. That was all it took for me, and with one last push, we reached ecstasy simultaneously. Cole carefully rolled over next to me.

"Wow! Every time we're together, Faith, you get me. A small ball of fire starts inside and gets bigger and bigger until I can't stand it anymore, and I want to be one with you," he said, almost out of breath.

"I know what you mean. The same thing happens to me. I've never experienced passion like this before."

We lay there, our naked bodies coiled together.

Suddenly, Cole sat up and said, "Oh my God, I smell smoke!" He jumped up and quickly put on his clothes.

"Smoke? What are you talking about?" I followed his lead and put on my clothes.

"I smell a fire. I need to see if I can help," Cole said, hugging me.

"If you're going, then I'm going with you!" *Weren't we on vacation?*

I held his hand, ran down the steps, and followed him out onto the street.

"I need to see if I can help," Cole chanted.

"But, we're on vacation," I pleaded.

"It's the strangest thing. When there's a fire, I have an instinct to help. I think it has something to do with being abandoned as a child."

We ran around the corner and into smoke. My eyes stung and I coughed. Smoke was everywhere!

Gaby's was on fire, and patrons were filtering out of the place screaming, "Call 911!"

"It must've just started," Cole said, trying to breathe. "Where are the damn fire trucks?"

"I hear them," I said, coughing.

Cole led me away from the scene and across the street.

"Stay right here. I need to go inside! I'm trained in this stuff. I'll be fine," he said. Then he quickly kissed me and said, "I love you!"

"But . . ." Before I could say more, he sprinted across the street and ran inside alone.

The sirens grew louder, and within minutes, fire trucks screeched to a halt. Firefighters in full gear quickly streamed out of the trucks and raced toward the building.

I ran over to one of the firefighters and yelled, "My boyfriend is a fireman and he just went inside to help!"

"Yes, ma'am. Stay here! We're going in," he yelled, and then said something into his radio.

A couple firefighters got out the long hose attached to the truck while others put on oxygen tanks and grabbed axes.

People nearby were hysterical, especially those filing out of the bar and into the dense smoke. I covered my mouth with my shirt and crouched down near the ground, remembering smoke rises.

In a panic, my brief relationship with Cole flashed across my mind. *We are on vacation! Why is Cole inside this blazing building? Where is he? Is he okay?* My heart pounded in my chest and my hands were sweaty. I heaved dry air. Time crawled in milliseconds. More hysteria set in. I had difficulty breathing and I couldn't stop coughing.

A police officer ran toward me. "You need to leave the area immediately! This place could potentially blow up," she yelled, trying to corral me to move.

"My boyfriend is inside! I don't know where he is!"

"The firefighters are doing all they can to get him out of there, but you can't stay here!"

"But . . ." It was no use explaining anything more to her. I could barely talk, and my throat was raw from smoke inhalation. There was only one thing I could do.

I sprinted across the street calling out Cole's name, but only croaked whispers resounded. *He has to come out! We just met! It can't end now, not after all we've been through! Oh God, get him out of there safely! Where the hell are you, Cole?*

I managed to run through the barricade of medics and as close to the front door as possible. Just then, I felt two hands forcibly grab me. I kicked and screamed. Somehow, I escaped the person's hold. At that moment, I looked up and saw a man stagger out of the front door.

I ran toward him, but the smoke was too thick. I stopped. My eyes stung and I couldn't see. I began to teeter and fall backwards. Someone caught me and carried me to the other side of the street.

The person gently put me on the ground. Then he fell down.

With my last ounce of strength, I yelled, "Cole!"

"Faith! Over here!" I looked next to me and saw a man coughing, covered with soot.

"Cole?" I recognized his buttoned-down shirt. "Oh my God! It's you!" I crawled over to him.

Cole groaned.

Oh no! Not now, God, please not now! Mama, please help! Don't take him from me!

"Faith . . ." As Cole's eyes started to flutter, he murmured, "I love you."

Dear Reader: Thank you for reading *Finding Faith*. I hope you enjoyed the twists and turns in Faith's journey. Honest reviews help keep me inspired to continue writing stories like this one.

Please consider leaving a review.
Thank you, Michelle

Printed in Great Britain
by Amazon

29147865R00129